The Stars Will Guide Us Back

RUE SPARKS

RUE SPARKS

CONTENT WARNINGS

Apocalypse/End of the World Scenario
Mentions of Toxic Masculinity
Cosmic Events
Depression & Anxiety
Domestic Violence (Off-screen/Implied)
Gaslighting
Grief & Loss
Homophobia (Verbal)
Mentions of Unsupportive Parenting
Terminal Illness

I remember the pinpricks of light,
breaking apart the dark abyss
that breathed cold air down our necks
from the car's sunroof.

We called out our joys and sorrows to the stars,
fingers clasped like knitted wool.
The road stretching ahead with possibilities,
the night filled with music from our lungs and hearts.

The memory is a haloed echo, the phantom of light
of an incandescent bulb as I close my eyes.
Like trying to remember your face
like it is in the photograph on my desk.

Sometimes it feels like the memories and photos
are all that I have left of you.
Other days, as my fingers tap the keys
I remember the gifts you gave me to survive your absence.

With the road stretching a lifetime ahead
only the ghost of a touch on my fingertips.
You remind me the night has its own music,
and the stars will guide us back to where we belong.

For my wife
1987-2017

TABLE OF CONTENTS

A NEW COLOR OF SUNRISE

I'VE BEEN STARING at my account for half an hour, but it doesn't change. No matter how much I will it, no money magically appears.

There's a new color. They say it is best viewed during sunset, though the sunrise is a close second. Like nothing anyone has seen before, they say.

"They said that about the last color too," I say to no one. It echoes off the rusted metal walls of my workshop, taking detours around crowbars and hammers, finding its end in the heat of the furnace.

They also said it about the last smell. The last touch. A few colors before were described as 'life-changing' and 'the greatest discovery of the millennia.'

Isolated in my shop, pounding away at wares for the fortunate and famous to decorate their lavish homes, I'd missed all of them.

The last color I missed because I got sick and lost several weeks of pay.

The new smell before that I missed when my brother broke his arm and needed a cast.

Before that, it was a leaky roof.

Before that, my bike needed repairs.

I blink three times in quick succession to close my account window, pull the NuSight glasses from my face, set them on the table.

No point in dreaming today.

Clients come and go, their chatter an abrasive staccato.

"Did you see the new color?" one asks. "Breathtaking, isn't it?"

"Can you paint it the new color?" is met with an unsatisfactory 'No,' costing me a consignment.

"Why ever not?" she asks, and I don't have it in me to explain about copyright and proprietary data.

When the bevy of clients evens out, I'm able to forget about the new color for the next several hours. It's a hot day, hotter still near the furnace. The sweat creeps down my face, my neck. I'm sure I'm covered in soot and dirt by the time the sun sets.

I allow myself to watch it, cooling myself off in the now-frigid air. I watch my *normal* sunset with the *normal* colors and try to not feel bitter.

New color or no, it's still beautiful.

I feel wrung out and sore when my alarm goes off the next morning, the sound grating. I'm brushing my teeth, still in a daze when I hear the high-pitched beeping of the glasses. I figure it may be a new client. I spit out the foamy toothpaste, go back to the bedroom where I'd left them.

It's from an address I don't recognize but takes up the whole screen. The message is one line, a sans serif font in red: "See What They *See*."

My head tells me to swipe it away, but my gut tells me to click on it.

I notice nothing new at first until I turn towards where the curtains block the window. There is a sliver of color, a halo around the reds and oranges peeking through the curtains.

I move quickly, nearly tripping over last nights' clothes in my hurry. I pull the curtains back. The sun is just making its way into the sky, surrounded by pinks, oranges—*and whatever it was they called the new color.*

For a moment, I only breathe. My thoughts become dim, muted in the sight. There are no words to describe it.

They said the sunrise was a close second?

I can't imagine a more beautiful sight than this.

When the hack is finally caught by the manufacturers, long after the sun has risen, the color leaves my sight. There is still a smile on my face.

"Did you see the new color?" a client asks later that day, and I shake my head with a crooked smile, the secret a precious thing reserved for only me.

The memory of the color will fade. But for a moment, I owned the world.

FEAR NOT THE GODS

I OFTEN WONDER what the gods thought would happen upon their return. Maybe they thought we needed guidance, that their magnanimous but firm hand would turn the human race into a thing of universal beauty.

They probably didn't expect a war. I wonder how omnipotent beings didn't see it coming. If there's one universal human trait, it's that we don't like to be told what we can and cannot be. Even by our creators.

But it's not the gods I fear. It's men.

"You cannot be serious?" I say through clenched teeth. My compatriot grimaces at my tone, baring his teeth in his annoyance. He turns away and continues setting the charge.

We're three hundred feet below street level in one of the gods' free cities. They're utopias where humanity enjoys equanimity and safety … provided they worship the hands that feed them.

"You think I got time to joke?" he says, straightening when the last one is ready and grabbing the roll of wire by the dowels on either side of the plastic base. He lets it loose as he walks backward. I follow behind him at a clip.

"I was told this was a reckon mission, not that we were going to blow up part of a city and all the citizens in it!" I rush forward, grab either side of the roll by the dowels so he can't keep moving away from me. "I did not agree to this."

"Of course you did," he says with a sneer, face smudged with dirt and grease from our trip into the undercity. "What, you think those people up there are innocent? They chose their side; now they can pay for it."

He tries to yank the roll back, but I hold tight. My voice is steel. "I. Did. Not. Agree. To. This."

He jerks the roll out of my hands, glaring daggers at me. "You didn't have to." The tone holds no room for argument. "You can do your duty or die with them."

He continues moving back, and after a moment I follow him.

I wait until we're out of sight of the charge, nearly out of the undercity, when in a moment of trust, he turns his back to me to pick up the pack we'd abandoned.

The shot from my pistol is muffled by the silencer. No echo to sound my betrayal, to sound the alarm for our troops nearby. The shot through his neck is an instant kill.

His body drops. I catch it, wary of setting off the still active charge. I'm debating my next move when I first hear, then feel the rumbling ground beneath my feet. There's a white-hot shot of fear in my chest as I remember the still active bomb in the undercity. I'm debating whether I have time to deactivate it before the earthquake sets it off, when the ground above my head is suddenly peeled back, as if the crust of the city were nothing but a thin layer of wrapping paper around me. I dodge rocks and bits of steel as debris falls.

When the sunlight strikes my eyes, I turn my face upward and face the God I knew had found me.

FOLLOW THE SUN

"PLACE THE ITEMS ON THE CLOTH," the witch instructs. "Align them with the heart in the center, the rest in a circle around. Let yourself feel where each piece belongs; they'll let you know."

Cienna is not so sure but does as she's told. The heart is the gold-plated fountain pen she had been gifted by her father long before he died. The other supplies she spreads around it: a rosebud from her family's garden where she grew up; her favorite childhood book, the pages yellowed, tattered, and spine creased; the last letter she received from her father; the obituary from her sister's death when she was a child.

With every item placed she closes her eyes and does as instructed, feeling where they belong in the circle. She places the remaining knick-knacks before letting out a drained sigh, surprised at how much effort it has taken to complete.

"Good," the witch whispers near her ear. "Now, remember, I told you this part requires sacrifice."

"The blood," Cienna says with a nod. "I'm willing to do what has to be done."

The witch's mouth twitches in a slight smile, her crow's feet crinkling in amusement at Cienna's eagerness. "Yes, that too. But remember, these items will be sacrificed as well. As will a part of you. Nothing comes from nothing, you understand? Are you certain of your path?"

Cienna breathes in the scent of mugwort and rose that wafts from the nearby incense, gaze hazy on the circle of items.

"Yes," she says. "My path is clear. This is what I was meant to do."

The witch nods and picks up a dagger from a table next to the altar. She gently takes Cienna's hand and makes a delicate slice along her finger. Cienna winces at the pain; for all that it's not deep, it bleeds quickly. The witch draws the finger along her own palm, a streak of blood remaining on the witch's hand.

The deed done, Cienna watches with horrified curiosity as the witch turns towards the altar and wraps the cloth over the items, one side then another, folding it inward over and over again as if there is nothing in the cloth at all. Until all that remains on the table is a small square of folded fabric.

There is a static hum in the room when the witch places her hand on the cloth and begins to speak.

"Where once there was pain, now there is lucidity. Where there was love, now is laid bare. Where shadow and light collide, there is truth."

The witch places her bloodied hand palm down on the altar cloth, and though nothing outwardly changes, Cienna feels a crushing in her chest that takes her breath away. The witch unfolds the cloth, and with each unfolding a jolt of pain runs through Cienna's veins like lightning. It isn't until the final unfolding that she's able to again breathe, ragged but with big gulps of blessed oxygen.

On the altar cloth now sits a leather-bound book.

"Is that it?" Cienna's asks breathlessly. "Did it really work?"

The witch picks up the book and brings it to Cienna. It's heavy in her hands, the volume thick. There's no title, but on the bottom of the cover, she sees the name of the author.

Cienna Eaton.

"It worked." Her words come out as a breath. "This book is mine."

"Of course it worked," the witch says as she straightens the altar cloth, smoothing it with her hands. "A book is made of all your loves, your hates, your pain, your joys. Whether you write it or magic it into being."

"I can't believe it." Cienna traces the book with her fingertips. "I can become published now. Like father always wanted."

The witch sighs, startling Cienna out of her awe. She looks up to meet the witch's gaze. The witch is looking at her with a furrowed brow, mouth in a thin line.

"What?" Cienna asks, but the witch only shakes her head.

It's when the witch is leading her to the threshold and Cienna is closing the door behind her that the witch does speak, holding the door open a fraction and whispering so Cienna has to lean forward to hear.

"A word of advice?"

"Yes?" Cienna asks.

"If you only ever follow the sun, you're going to get burned."

THE WILD

THE DRESS IS DECORATED with fine embroidery and small, glittering gems along the edges, all tulle and fine silk, billowing up in the skirt and fitted on the waist, torso, and quarter sleeves. It's a jeweled sapphire, sure to stand out in the finest of courts, even the stylized drawing a jaw-dropping testament to the finest royal fashion can be.

He instantly hates it.

"You can't be serious," Clay says. "That's going to cost a fortune. And for what, a weekend? That's ridiculous, Kim. Don't do it."

Kim grabs the color copy from where Clay is wrinkling it between his fingers in clear exasperation. She sets it on the table to lay it flat and smooth out the wrinkles with her fingers.

"This isn't just *any* weekend, Clay. It's the biggest cosplaying event in the country! All the big names will be there. It's my chance to stand out as a seamstress, to make a name for myself. If I pull this off, I could *double* my follower count easily, maybe even triple!"

Clay rubs fingers into his eye sockets and lets out a loud exhale. "Kim. Do you even have the money for this?"

There is a telling pause where Kim taps her fingers against the table and avoids Clay's gaze.

"Well. It could be worse. But I'll have to borrow money from my parents. And well … that's what I wanted to talk to you about."

Clay straightens. "Absolutely not."

"But Clay—"

He stands from the kitchen table quickly enough to send his chair squealing against the floor. "No. I am not funding a dress you're going to wear for three nights so you can run around pretending to be a princess when you could, I don't know, spend that money on replacing that junker you drive or save the money for the next time your heater blows."

"One." Kim says, arms crossed.

"What?"

"One night. I can't wear the same costume more than one day. It's not done."

Clay's mouth opens and closes as he stares at his brown-eyed auburn-haired girlfriend before he shakes his head.

"Are you *crazy*?! You're acting completely ridiculous. Stop trying to relive some childhood fantasy and grow up."

It is the wrong thing to say. Kim gathers up her papers and her bag, avoiding Clay's gaze as her mouth sets firm. Clay considers apologizing, but he meant everything he said.

Clay throws up his arms as the echo of the side door banging shut ends the conversation. His fingers grip his tawny hair, pulls at the sides until his eyes ache with it.

Letting go, he scratches through his hair, shaking his head. He drags his feet towards the hallway. He can still feel the anger tight in his chest, a confined lion pacing, itching for a fight, a meal.

As he steps into the beige nineties carpet of the hallway, he can see the rough bark and silky, vibrant green leaves of trees bursting through the stained fibers. It masks the awful egg-white walls he swears he is going to paint over someday—they disappear behind the canvas of his own personal jungle.

By the time he makes his way into his man-cave, the second-to-last door on the right, he is pushing through the stringy undergrowth that clings to his ankles. That is okay, though. He knows the way well.

He pulls off a few brave vines that have tried to reclaim his office chair as their own, stubbornly gripping the small pieces that have gotten into the casters of the wheels.

He rolls it a couple of times, making sure nothing remains in the creases, then sits into his plush, lumbar-supporting chair and pulls up to his kingdom. A click of the mouse and the sun rises into his domain when the monitor comes to life.

He no longer jumps at the first feelings of the cold, briny water touching his toes. He digs in his heels and sits in his chair until the first mast and sail rise behind him. The sand under his toes is soon replaced by the splintered and worn wood of a ship long-loved, having sailed to distant shores and back many times.

The waters, now leagues deep, camouflage his desktop tower, the spider plant his girlfriend had been attempting to save and the mountain of bills that are stacked haphazardly to the right side of his desk. As they are lost to his sight, they drift from his mind like so much sea trash.

He pulls out his compass and map, sets sail for where the Wild reign.

—

Clay looks again, but the space-suit clad astronaut with the 'Happy 30th Birthday' balloon waiting for their copies at the printer doesn't disappear.

He barks out a laugh, which earns him a glare from across his computer monitor from Jessica. She looks up at him with cold green eyes below perfectly stenciled eyebrows before looking back down at her screen. Clay sweeps the room with his gaze, but no one else notices the astronaut. No one seems to see anything out of the ordinary at all.

I'm being pranked, he thinks, and picks up his phone to take a casual photo of the astronaut as they pick their copies up from the tray in their thickly gloved fingers before they move down the hall, the white balloon with the rainbow text cheerily bobbing behind them.

"Clay, I needed that report yesterday!" his boss calls from the fishbowl room next to him, and Clay quickly becomes entranced in his job, forgetting about the strange astronaut for the remainder of the morning.

—

The firefighter is next.

Needless to say, coming into the breakroom and seeing a firefighter fully clad in mustard yellow, soot covered gear instantly puts Clay on edge, but after seeing the quality of the astronaut gear, and upon recognizing Matthew from the IT department behind the mask, his mood turns from panicked, takes a quick stop at confused, and settles on careful amusement. *They're really dedicated to this prank. Should I play along or call them out?*

Matthew is opening packets of sugar to add to his coffee—a somewhat incongruous vision considering his attire—when Clay sidles up to him, feigning innocence. He reaches for the coffee pot and pours himself a cup as well.

"So. Put out any fires lately?"

Matthew chuckles low, reaches into the fridge for the creamer, and adds a healthy dose, though he nearly drops it through his thick gloves.

"You have no idea. Nancy in sales downloaded a PDF from an unknown sender, and it downloaded a virus onto her computer and nearly wiped it. We could have had a serious security issue on our hands if she hadn't realized her mistake and turned the computer off immediately. Why, imagine if we'd been liable for ..."

Matthew drones on, and Clay stirs his coffee with a growing frown on his face, one that Matthew misses in his excitement. He gesticulates when he talks, leading him to spill coffee on his thick, soot-stained coat. It doesn't make much of a stain, but Matthew drops his coffee cup in the sink immediately and searches frantically for a paper towel.

"You can barely see it," Clay comments, handing Matthew a few napkins. He immediately wets them and begins tenderly dabbing at the stain.

"I can't have a stain, not today! I'm meeting my fiancée's parents after work. Besides that, Jenna will kill me, this shirt is organic silk! Ugh." He turns to Clay, holding his arms out, displaying the full ensemble of firefighter regalia, complete with a tool belt including an axe that Clay hadn't noticed before. *How was he allowed to bring that in here? If I'm being punked, these are some extreme lengths they're going to. Better to stop it here.*

"You look like a firefighter, Matthew. I don't think they're going to notice a coffee stain."

Confusion and anxiety twist Matthew's face as he re-wets the napkins and starts dabbing at the spot again. The rough fabric shreds the napkin, leaving small spots of white pulp where it has come apart.

"What? Oh hell, I knew we shouldn't have gone with the mustard color. It looks that bad? We thought the dark gray fitted pants would offset it." He throws the napkins into the trash and rubs at his face.

"I probably look like a Grey Poupon bottle. We bought a green one too, hopefully I won't look like relish. I'll change before I get home."

Matthew starts walking towards the door but pauses to pat Clay on the shoulder. "Thanks for the heads up. You're quiet, but you're a good guy. Appreciate it."

Before he disappears through the doorway, Clay calls him back.

"So, you didn't dress as a firefighter on purpose?"

Matthew chuckles and scratches at his chin with his thick glove, soot streaking his face as it blossoms into a half smile. "You know, I always wanted to be one. But that was a long time ago. People change. Realism won out I guess."

He shrugs and disappears through the doorway, leaving Clay stranded in the breakroom on his own with his confusion and anxiety twisting in his chest.

What the ever-loving fuck?

—

When their director of sales is dressed as a ballerina, Clay is officially past amused and solidly settled in the realm of concerned for his health. The director, Lyle, begins the meeting doing stretches, and during the presentation they perform poses in front of the projector screen, complete with skin-tight black leotard covered in an array of blue and purple sequins that sparkle like starlight. They wear black tights, sky blue pointed toe shoes laced up their calves.

When Clay risks a glance around the room, the rest of the sales team is preoccupied on their laptops, taking notes or scrolling social media. None of them seem phased as Lyle touches their right foot in an arc near to the back of their head as they discuss the decrease in sign-ups the past quarter.

"While we've seen an increase in customer loyalty and satisfaction with our customer service, we're struggling to meet our goals in new customer relations." They pirouette as they continue. Clay wonders at their ability to do so in a confined space and maintain their professional tone at the same time.

With a twirl and bow, Lyle clicks to the final slide. "Any questions?"

Clay bites his tongue. He has questions alright, but he knows if he is going to question Lyle it has to be one on one. If his suspicions are correct, and he is the only one who can see these strange getups, then he can't let on about his personal gnosis.

Lyle fields a few questions about the particulars of the new registration regulations before dismissing the meeting. A few of his colleagues approach Lyle with comments, leaving Clay to lean against the wall and tap his foot as his thoughts spiral and he waits for an opening to talk to them alone.

Finally, they are the last people in the room. When Lyle begins removing the cords from their laptop connecting it to the projector, Clay approaches them.

"That was … some performance," he says, internally thrashing himself. *Smooth.*

Lyle snorts. They have always been professional in meetings and during work hours but have a snarky streak that shows its face when one on one.

"It was a quarterly debriefing. Hardly my finest hour." They shut their laptop and hold it to their chest before they turn to him, winged eyeliner contrasting their light gray eyes and highlighting their buzzed black hair. "Did you need something Clay?"

"Yeah, actually. My girlfriend was interested in taking ballet, and I heard you might have some connections."

Lyle looks taken aback, head jerking backward for a moment and confusion infiltrating their gaze. "Where the hell'd you hear that?"

Clay shrugs, feigning ignorance. "Through the grapevine."

Lyle scrunches up their face, silent for a moment before answering. "I haven't been involved in ballet for a long, long time. Not since I was a kid. I won't be much help. Sorry."

Lyle pushes past him, jostling Clay's shoulder in an uncharacteristically clumsy moment.

"Hey, wait!" Clay follows them through the doorway and down the hall towards their office.

Lyle stops and turns. "What, Clay? I have to get to a meeting."

"Why'd you stop?"

"Stop what?" they ask, annoyance in their tone.

"Ballet."

They turn away from him and stare at the neutral gray wall. "Not that it's any of your business, but my father didn't approve. That's more than I should be telling you." They walk down the hall, and Clay lets them.

As he walks back to his desk, he tries to focus on his predicament, but there is something about Lyle's face that unsettles him.

Someone shouldn't give up on their dreams on someone else's say so.

The thought settles like a lead ball of guilt in his stomach.

—

The Wild is unruly tonight. The seas are a furious, thrashing miasma that reaches over the ship's rails and soaks his socks, but Clay ignores the sea water between his toes and clicks the mouse furiously, centers on the visage of an armored orc in the crossfire.

"Die, damnit!" he mutters as the screen flashes, signaling the damage he takes. "You shouldn't be at this level on this island."

The orc doesn't listen, striking at Clay's character on the computer monitor. Despite his misgivings, Clay decides on using one of his precious bombs to make a crushing blow against the monster, setting it down and counting down to eight before running in the opposite direction of the orc, far enough to escape the blast but not early enough for the orc to do the same.

"Yes," Clay whispers, careful not to wake Kim. Though the lightning and thunder should have kept her awake, if not the groaning of the sails and the wood beneath his feet, the Wild is a secret all Clay's own.

I'm not ashamed of it, per se. I don't want her calling me a hypocrite.
He doesn't linger on the thought that she might be right.

As he picks up his bounty, his thoughts wander instead to the strangeness of the day. *An astronaut, a firefighter, and a ballerina walk into a bar,* but the joke, and the question of what it means, has no conclusion he can come up with.

After looting the rest of the island, he sets sail for another bounty, eyes peeled for any unwary ship or land formation he can reap the rewards from. *The pirate's life for me.* He ignores the guilt and unsettled feelings that run from the back of his neck down his spine.

Maybe things will be back to normal in the morning.

—

Things aren't back to normal in the morning.

Pam, their secretary who sits at the front desk and greets everyone as they come in, is dressed as a veterinarian, wearing scrubs with subtle light blue paw-prints and carrying a stethoscope around her neck.

Clay notices Dave in customer service is dressed in the gold and red silks of a horse jockey, a black, hard cap clinched around his chin and wearing knee-high boots. He slaps a riding crop against his leg as he leans on the partition wall, chatting with Fiona, who is dressed as a race car driver, black jumpsuit covered in sponsor patches and a helmet sitting next to her laptop on her desk.

Clay tries to keep his head faced forward as he escapes to the water cooler at the first opportunity, only to see Sam sitting at the table looking at his phone, his bulking, muscled frame in a football uniform. Not being a football fan, Clay can't recognize the blue and silver colors of the team, but the black padded shoulders and tight white pants seem familiar. *A local team maybe?*

He considers evading Sam completely, but he sighs in defeat.

There's really nowhere to escape. Clay grabs a styrofoam cup and fills it at the water dispenser, sips at the cool liquid and avoids Sam's gaze.

There is a sigh, a few moments of silence, and a curse. *Don't get involved.* But he wonders what else there is to do. *Either I slowly lose my mind or I take the hint.*

"Something wrong?" he asks Sam, circling around the table so he faces the other man, curled over his phone. It is a strange sight, someone so strong and defined yet so defeated.

"Wishful thinking," Sam says, not looking up from his phone. "You know how it is." He shrugs, sets his phone down and sips at his own cup.

Clay considers his options. *Clearly there's something I'm meant to do. That or I've really lost my mind.*

He sits down and sets his cup of water on the table. "Guess I don't know how it is. What you wishing for?"

Sam leans back, and Clay realizes there are black streaks of face paint under his eyes. He's seen it on other football players before but doesn't know the purpose. *I might be out of my league in this one.*

"My kid wants to quit football. It's pissing me off. Or maybe choking me up." He shrugs, then chuckles to himself. "I didn't get that choice. Can't believe I'm saying this, but I'm jealous of my own kid."

Clay raises his eyebrows at that. "Why didn't you have the choice?"

"I got injured in high school, messed up my left knee. I would have had a full ride to college if not for that. Coulda had a career in it. But sometimes things don't work out the way we want them to, I guess." Sam grabs his cup, chugs down the water, then tosses the cup towards the trash can. A perfect shot.

He stands and shakes his head. "But you can't force your dreams and wants on others. That's not how life works. He wants to play soccer, so he'll get to play soccer. He's still the best thing that's ever happened to me. Even if I didn't get to play football, I still have the best kid a dad could ask for. That's worth more than any Super Bowl win."

Clay frowns as he swirls the water in his cup, deep in thought. "But that dream meant everything to you."

Sam shrugs. "Sometimes it's not the dream itself, it's what it makes you. I wanted to be somebody. When you're a dad, you're everything to somebody. Seems like I got the better deal."

Clay rubs a hand over his eyes, confusion marring his thoughts. "But what about …?"

Sam turns back from where he's been walking away. "What about what?"

Clay shakes his head, dazed. "Nothing; never mind. Thanks for the advice."

Sam smiles at him, all teeth, then leaves.

Clay's heart pounds in his chest. For those last moments, when he'd looked back up at Sam, instead of the football uniform, he'd been in his standard button up and khaki's. As if it were any other day.

What the hell is going on?

—

It takes everything Clay has to not stare slack jawed.

It is one of the most elaborate costumes yet, and definitely the most unexpected. Ian, one of his colleagues on the sales team and their resident asshole, is dressed as the epitome of a knight in shining armor. The ornate metal helmet falls low over his brow, obscuring his face except for the narrowed eyes and pompous smirk. Red feathers reach towards the ceiling from the helmet's peak, fluttering in the wind from the overhead fan.

The worst part of the whole situation though are the words coming out of his mouth, which are decidedly not very knight-like.

"That is the biggest load of bull I have ever heard," Clay says in reply, not holding back. He and Ian don't get along at the best of times and are at each other's throats at the worst of times. The meeting is a terrible idea, made worse by Clay's current predicament.

"It's a great idea, and I've already run it by Yuna. All I need is your agreement to run it by upper management. Come on Clay. Don't be jealous because you didn't think of it first."

Clay bites down on his tongue as the fury bubbles up his throat. He grits his teeth against his more colorful replies.

"Legal will never agree to this. And even if they do, it's wrong. This completely takes advantage of our older clientèle's lack of understanding of modern technology and current legal practices."

Ian shrugs and shuffles the papers they've gone over in front of him. The metal armor clinks awkwardly as he moves. "That's not my problem."

Clay throws his arms in the air. "Not to mention this will be a customer service nightmare! Do you know how many customers will complain about missing the fine print? Our approval ratings will tank! You can't be serious, Ian."

Ian smiles shrewdly. "That's their problem, not sales."

Clay breathes deeply and glares at Ian, the force of his anger a storm in his chest. *What can I do to make him understand?*

As Ian taps the table, the metal on his fingers making a harsh clang with every hit, a thought surfaces.

"It's not very chivalrous."

Ian looks up at Clay, an eyebrow raised barely visible beneath the helmet's rim. "Pardon?"

"This plan. It's not very knight-like. Would one of King Arthur's Knights of the Round Table really use such under-handed tactics?"

Ian's face screws into a frown. "What does that have to do with anything?"

Clay sighs and leans on his elbows. "Look, Ian. I know this isn't you. This persona, this guy who doesn't care about anything but the bottom line. I know you weren't always this way. What happened to the kid who wanted to do the right thing? Who played at ascending to knighthood, of being the hero?"

Ian stares into Clay's eyes, unblinking. "Where did you even hear that?"

Clay smiles. "It's there if you know where to look."

Ian is unamused, eyes narrowing as he leans back and crosses thickly gauntleted arms awkwardly over his armored chest. The sight would be comical if it weren't for the sword Clay could see in its scabbard at his waist. "You think you're funny? Whenever have I given the impression that I cared more about anything other than myself?"

At least he knows he's a selfish ass. Clay tries another tactic.

"It can't have *started* like that. Surely something had to have happened down the line to change your mind about things. I know you have it in you to be the hero, Ian. You have to let yourself see it too."

Ian looks down at the papers, shuffles a few. "You're not wrong," he says, not looking in Clay's eyes. "I always aspired to be the hero." He frowns, then gathers them into a pile, made all the more difficult by the gauntlets. "But that was a long time ago. People change. I doubt I'd even know how to be the hero if I tried."

Clay is tempted to take Ian at his words, but there's something about the tone that speaks of an undercurrent of longing.

Ian stands when he's finally stacked the papers in one arm and balanced his laptop in his other hand and starts heading towards the door with a careful clanking.

"Ian, wait," Clay calls out and doesn't give him the chance to decide to ignore him. "You know, part of being the hero is deciding who you want to be."

Ian pauses, halfway out the door, and Clay continues, "You don't have to be a knight. But there was something about being them that you aspired to. Even if you can't be the hero, maybe just this once, you can do the right thing."

Ian doesn't respond, and the door closes with a barely audible click.

Later that day, Clay gets an email from Yuna that Ian has removed his proposal from the queue, and Clay is unsurprised when he looks up at a passing Ian to see him sporting his typical cardigan and black pants.

—

The Wild is sunshine and calm seas, and Clay can't figure it out. *It's never been like this. I'm not sure what I'm supposed to do here.*

When he had landed on the shore of an island, he had expected to be attacked by orcs, trolls, and goblins, but instead, he found remains of ancient civilizations that hosted only the occasional worthless relic and mismatched set of tools or clay pots.

He wanders the whole island in a daze without any combat, loot, or traps before giving up and boarding his ship. The sun beats down on the wooden deck, warming his face and forcing him to squint along the horizon.

There are no ships and few land masses. There are no dangerous sea creatures or dragons to be bested.

And yet, Clay feels a sense of belonging that far outweighs the reckless abandon he always feels in the Wild. It's as if he's in a waking dream, a settled contentment he's not experienced since childhood.

Can we twist our dreams somewhere along the lines? he wonders.

He has no answer, so he does what he knows best; he sets sail to a new horizon. But this time, he does so with an open heart.

—

"Clay?"

"I'm in here! Kim's home; you'll have to say 'hi,'" Clay says to his mom on the laptop screen. "It's been a while since you two had a chat."

Kim slinks into the living room, arms crossed and a dour expression on her face. *Still angry at me. I don't blame her.*

When she sidles up next to him her expression changes. *Probably for Mom's sake.* "Hello Gwen," Kim says with a small wave. "How are you doing? It's been a while."

"Oh, lovely, now I see your face! I hope you're keeping Clay in line. He needs someone like you to keep him looking up." Gwen's smile is wide, her short white hair framing large black plastic glasses over brown eyes. She's in a folding chair in front of a well-maintained garden, her pride and joy.

"The garden looks lovely," Kim says, a genuine smile on her face. "And you know how Clay is. Stubborn," she says, elbowing him, "but he has his own charm."

Gwen laughs, and Clay rubs at his side where Kim elbowed him harder than necessary. *I deserved that.*

"He is that. Which is why I was so surprised to hear from him! We usually have our calls twice a month like clockwork, but here he calls me out of the blue. You wouldn't have anything to do with that, would you?"

Kim's eyebrows furrow, and she steals a glance at Clay. "No, actually. I'm as surprised as you are."

Gwen's smile softens as she looks at her son. "Well, that does surprise me. And we've been having such a wonderful conversation at that. Do you want to tell her what you asked me, or should I?"

Clay shrugs, avoiding both of their gazes and shoves his hands in his pockets. "I asked what my childhood dreams were."

Kim snorts, then blinks in confusion when he doesn't react. "Wait, seriously? You, asking about childhood dreams?"

Clay shrugs and bites at his lip. "I can't quite remember what they were. Mom was enlightening me."

"He had so many when he was young, but once he hit six it was the same one, year after year. But he was so shy, he would only share it with the people he trusted the most. Maybe he was afraid people would laugh at him; I don't rightly know."

Kim smiles and encircles Clay's arm with her own, leaning into his side.

"I think that's sweet."

"Anyway, I must be going, but please stay in touch, both of you. I'll talk to you on our monthly call?"

Clay nods, finger hovering over the mouse. "Of course."

"Ta!" Gwen says, then disconnects, Clay following suit.

When Clay leans back from the laptop, Kim turns him towards her, setting her hands on his shoulders. "So. Your childhood dreams, huh?"

Clay sighs and clasps her hands within his own. "You were right, Kim. I was wrong to judge you."

Kim leans back in surprise. "What?"

"You deserve to be treated like a princess," Clay continues. "And a ninja, and a fairy, and a catgirl. Whatever you want to be, I'll support you."

Kim grabs his chin and tilts his face towards her, so they lock gazes.

"No more complaining about the cosplay?"

Clay smiles. "None. Except when I step on beads or leather tacks, then I reserve the right to complain that they're on the floor."

"Deal."

It is later, after Kim has finished brushing her teeth and is headed to the bed they sometimes share that Clay risks a look into the mirror.

He looks first into his own brown eyes and rusty brown hair. Slowly, he lets his gaze travel down his torso towards his clothing, and a smile forms.

Some dreams change.

Some could be reborn.

WATCH AS I FLY

THE DREAM IS ALWAYS the same.

The feel of the wind is like a balm — it soothes an itch beneath her skin. The cool air blows back her short-cropped hair to her skull. Her eyelids squint tight around her eyes, caught in the blossoming freedom of flying free. The sting of the wind tastes less like danger and more like home. Her clothes cling tight in front of her and loose and wild behind her as they whip and billow in the passing air.

She is flying. Not within the confines of an airplane, not falling like a skydiver or even gliding on a parachute. She is flying of her own accord, her own power, her own whim.

The feeling fills her lungs to bursting.

—

"I had that dream again," Joy says at breakfast. She swirls the dingy milk in her cereal bowl, now filled with the dredges of cinnamon and granola crumbs. The spoon clinks noisily against the side of the bowl, and though she winces at the noise, she continues. "It's going to be one of those days I guess."

"*Joyful* thoughts, Joy," Moira says between sips of her tea, perfectly lined lips leaving traces of crimson lipstick on the edges. Her fingers tap at her phone, eyes focused on the slim screen. "You manifest the energy you put out."

If only, maybe you'd look my way, Joy thinks but doesn't say out loud. Two years together, six months past moving in, and only Moira's dedication to perfection—a place for everything, even love—keeps their hearts sutured together.

"It's always like this," Joy mutters, not sure if she's talking about Moira's absent-mindedness or her prophetic dreams of an abysmal day.

Moira doesn't look up from her phone, her reply a distracted monotone. "There are no absolutes. There's no such thing as always or never. Remember what your therapist said."

Joy lets go of her spoon, and the sound as it clatters against the bowl makes her jump. She grabs her elbows with either hand, her fingers chilled from the cereal bowl. She cocoons her head deeper in her jumper but says nothing. She watches the clouds pass by in the ceiling-height windows, imagines the dragon-shaped one setting fire to the kitchen table and wonders whether that would warrant a glance her way if it did.

I hang out with too many eight-year-olds, she thinks, and takes her cereal bowl to the sink.

—

She flies over streets lined with lights twinkling as if on strings in the distance, the darkness of the ocean an abyss below her that doesn't scare her but makes her feel like the rest of the world is only an anthill for her to tread on if she so chose.

When she flies closer to the city, she can hear the shouts and exclamations of the crowd below, and it only reminds her of everything they lack, all she now possesses.

But that is not how the dream ever ends.

—

When Joy became a teacher, she thought having summers off for the rest of her life as an eternal blessing, the infinite equalizer that made all the madness of the school year seem *worth it*. In reality, summer means free time, which for Joy means boredom. She has few friends, fewer which are available during the time of year when most of them have vacations and family time.

You have to have family to have family time I suppose, Joy thinks, dropping her phone onto the couch cushion again. The steady thump of the repeated action feels cathartic, if pointless.

She is sprawled on the beige sectional in the living room, legs at a ninety-degree angle so her feet can cling precariously to the ottoman where the remotes sit uselessly. She'd long since tired of Netflix and Hulu. The noonday light shines through the large skylight in the living room ceiling and the large picture windows along the walls. It is a beautiful room, in a beautiful house.

She hates it.

A sudden bang and Joy lets go of her phone too soon. It clatters onto the wood floor, sliding under the legs of the ottoman. She winces, then looks around. Moira wasn't meant to be home for hours, yet the sound came from nearby.

Joy stands up shakily, heart still pounding rapidly from the sudden noise. She looks around the walls, thinking perhaps a painting or photo fell from a nail. Nothing.

She walks through the living room, peeks through the kitchen, the hallway, through the patio doors to be safe. Still, nothing.

"Get it together, Joy," she urges herself, and flops back down onto the sofa, the sudden drop reverberating through her bones. She lets out a sigh, facing up towards the ceiling and the skylight.

She blinks once, twice, and squints her eyes to focus on the high ceiling.

There's a bird perching on the seam of the skylight, staring down its jet-black beak at her.

—

As she flew, the wind lost its power, twisting from mighty to meek. At first, she finds herself flying lower. Then, instead of flying, she is making great leaps from building to building.

The cruelest moment is when only she is convinced she can fly at all. The people around her shake their heads, others laughing cynically or cruelly. Disbelieving and pitying.

It's in that moment of having had something grand and now knowing only its loss that she wakes up.

—

The ladder leaning against the outer wall of the house staggers underneath her feet, and Joy twists her hips to try and stay upright. Her heart flutters, and she grips the cracked wood so hard she feels the sting of splinters.

When the ladder steadies, she risks looking up, and sure enough, the bird is still there. "I can't believe I'm doing this. What's wrong with me? You better not shit on that window you damn thing! It'll be hell to clean off, you know!"

At first, Joy was surprised to see a bird perched on the skylight. It cawed at her, a throaty, brittle sound that made her shiver. The longer it stood there, though, the more she realized that something must be wrong. Most likely the bird had flown into the skylight, which was at an angle, and it was either dazed or injured.

She called Animal Control, but they had only said to let the bird take its time. Joy knew better, though; a storm was coming, and while the bird wasn't likely to get hurt by a little rain, if it were to fall from the roof, it may not survive the impact.

She debated calling Moira but quickly dismissed the thought as nonsense.

"Stay still!" Joy calls out, more to keep her own nerves in check than anything else. She is almost to the edge of the roof, the ladder she'd leaned against the wall steadier now that she isn't at the midpoint where she can't touch the building. Her knees feel weak, her hands sting from the splinters, and she feels woozy—but she is almost there.

When she reaches the top, she leans forward to place her hands, then her knees, then her toes on the roof. The rough tiles scrape at the palms of her hands, but she is thankful for their grip. She is on a part of the roof with a slightly different angle than the skylight, one side over.

She starts to inch her way towards the bird, where it is now cawing loudly and consistently, staring at her with black beady eyes. There are no other noises, even the other birds silent, presumably not wanting to become involved in the drama.

"Stop your yapping," she says. The wind kicks her dark hair into her eyes, and she mutters under her breath how thankful she is that she didn't let Moira convince her to keep it long. "I'm coming, I'm coming."

When she reaches the corner of the roof where the angle changes, she rolls onto her back, feet flat against the roof tiles. The sudden change in view sends her mind reeling; she peers over the edge, and the view of the tree line catches her off guard.

"This is … higher than I remember," she says to no one but the bird. The bird only caws in reply.

After the dizziness passes, she decides to go back onto her hands and knees, not liking the view. Her palms are sore, the gritty texture of the tiles cutting into her hands now, but she presses on.

She's a foot away from the bird—when it flies off. "You bastard!" Joy cries.

It's then that she loses her footing.

The roof tiles slide away before her eyes, and then she's flying.

———

She knows they see her. She knows because she hears the gasps, the screams, the yells, the calls. There's confusion, for sure, some whoops, still more screams. No one knows what to make of her, and the thought sends a thrill to her fingertips.

She flies between the high rises, daringly ghosts her fingers along the glass windows of a skyscraper as she whizzes up along it. She laughs when she reaches the top and allows herself to touch one sneaker to the tallest point before free-falling halfway down just to feel the flush on her skin.

———

Joy awakes to an itching on the back of her neck and stinging palms. She blinks back spots when she opens her eyes, using her palm to shade them from the orange glow of the sun. A sun that's much further down the horizon than she remembers.

She turns onto her side. There's nothing but freshly mowed grass and crushed leaves, sticking to her face, clothes, and hair. She wipes one arm across her mouth, sputtering out dirt and blades of grass. "What the hell?"

She looks up and sees the ladder leaned against the house and remembers.

The bird. The ladder. The roof. The flying.

Or more likely, the fall.

She pushes herself up on shaky legs, which tingle with pin-pricks as they come alive. She can taste the bitterness of old spit and greenery along with the grittiness of dirt in her mouth. She knows she's lucky not to be injured—not too much, at least—but she feels a fool. *Of course the bird didn't need my help*, she thinks. *No one does.*

After cleaning out the scratches on her hands with cold water and soap, she checks her phone, which thankfully wasn't cracked in the fall. Moira is late getting home, which for once is a gift rather than an annoyance. The scrapes on her hands would be a challenge to explain away, but not impossible. Being found knocked out in the grass? That would have been an ambulance ride for sure.

She gingerly lays down on the couch, careful with her aching shoulder and back. She glares at the offending skylight; the bird is nowhere to be seen. There's no indication there had been anything amiss at all. She knows she will have to remove the ladder tomorrow, but it's at the side of the house out of the way so Moira shouldn't see it coming home. Once that deed is done, it will be as if nothing happened. Utterly normal.

She pulls out her phone, unsurprised to see no missed calls, and only one text. It's from her friend Azalea, who's on vacation in California. She opens it, sure to find more photos of surfing, or white-water rafting, or some other nonsense, but the message is short: "does this remind you of someone? Dish, what have you been up to?!" with a link.

She's opening it without really registering or caring about what it could possibly be. Her and Azalea get on well enough, but it feels like a friendship of convenience rather than true connection. Still, watching a video from a friend is better than not-rescuing a not-injured bird from the roof.

What Joy sees has her sitting up suddenly on the sectional, grasping at her chest through her t-shirt.

There, in the midst of marshmallow clouds in a beautiful blue sky, flying between two skyscrapers, is a woman.

A woman who looks a lot like Joy.

—

She kicks up again into flight, spins in the air, legs tight together, feet in points as if she were a ballerina. The wind fights her, but she's stronger, her bones like steel against its hands as it tries to grab at her and fling her against the buildings.

Nothing can touch her.

—

"This is stupid," Joy says, even as she climbs.

She steadied the ladder deeper into the ground before she started climbing this time. The ladder creaks and jerks under her but stays against the wall of her home. Her handhold is more certain this time, her grip raw with determination.

She ignores the sting of a few new splinters, barely registering the pain. The wind blows softer than yesterday, tousling her hair lightly as she climbs. It's quiet, no cawing of the bird, but few songbirds. Their home isn't close enough to anyone to hear many neighbors either—something that has been a bonus for Moira, a detriment to Joy.

Joy grapples with the edge of the roof, then lays her palms flat on the tiles. This time, she bends her knees to stand with her feet flat against the roof tiles, determined not to crawl like she did yesterday.

"This is stupid," Joy repeats, a mantra now that does nothing to deter her from her goal. She walks towards the edge of the roof, where she'd fallen—flown—off the day before. Her legs shake, and she holds her arms out to steady her gait. There's a war in her chest between the butterflies of excitement in her stomach and the chilling fumes of fear in her lungs.

She stops a foot from the edge, looking down at the ground. She's only a story high, but with the height of their ceilings, that doesn't mean much.

"What am I even supposed to do?" she mutters between chattering teeth. "How did I do it last time?"

She closes her eyes and tries to remember. She'd been angry at first, then shocked, and then afraid. It had all happened in a split second. *Maybe I need to concentrate on my fear,* she thinks. *Or jump. But if I jump, I'll surely fall anyway. Maybe I should have tried hovering on the ground first?*

With her eyes closed, she focuses on the fear, that moment when she knew she was going to fall. Should she risk another fall? There has to be a better way.

Instead, she focuses on the fear in the current moment. The trembling of her fingers, the prickles in her fingertips. The weak feeling in her knees and the numbness in her feet. The ache from bending forward for so long to keep her balance. The vertigo she feels looking down. The pain in her chest, back, and head from yesterday's fall. The anger she'd felt at the bird for scaring her, the betrayal when she realized she was going to fall, to be in pain, because she'd tried to do the right thing.

She opens her eyes and looks down. She smiles.

—

It's a different dream this time.

She's falling. The wind isn't soothing or comforting, but rather it gnashes at her cheeks and scrapes at her hands and arms. It pulls back her legs and twists her at her waist. It pulls her clothes tight until she feels like she's being choked. She can't breathe, the wind filling her mouth, the taste bitter on her tongue, and numbing her teeth. Her eyes shut tight against the burn.

—

Moira is driving like a demon, whipping along the curves and straightaways with abandon, tight-lipped and a white-knuckled grip on the steering wheel.

"If you would just listen-"

Moira holds up a hand, palm towards her, a sure signal for silence. "I did listen, Joy, and it's crazy talk. You cannot fly, no one can fly, and I'm very concerned about you. Your therapist and I decided this is for the best."

Joy squeezes her fingers into fists in her lap, tight enough to feel crescent-shaped indentations in her palms. Her teeth ground tight and she scrunches up her face against the sting in her eyes. "You said you wouldn't use that word. *Crazy.*"

Moira sighs next to her, but she doesn't look. Joy holds her breath against the spots of gray dancing behind her closed eyelids. *She wouldn't even look at the video.*

"I did promise that. I'm sorry. But Joy, this is enough. We've dealt with your moods before, but this is different. You're hallucinating. They'll help you."

When Joy opens her eyes, she blinks against the tears threatening to fall, against the dizziness as Moira slows down before an SUV cuts them off exiting the parking lot to the beach. It would be another twenty minutes to get to her therapist's office on the opposite edge of the city from their suburban home. A plan begins to form, and Joy inches her left hand towards the buckle of her seatbelt.

"I'm not hallucinating. You aren't listening. I tried to show you the videos, but you wouldn't even look! You want to talk about my therapist? She said you're supposed to spend more time with me, *listen to me,* but you won't even try. You're always on your phone or gone, or too busy, and now when it really counts, you won't even give me a chance to explain myself."

There's that sigh again, and it's like the drop of a hammer. Joy times it perfectly. She waits for a stop sign, then swiftly unclips her seatbelt and opens the door. In a second, she's bolted and is running towards the entryway of a beach-side park.

"Joy!" She hears the scream but doesn't stop.

—

She's falling and there's no one to catch her. No one sees her. No one notices. There are no bystanders pointing up at the sky, no gasping or screaming for help. There's no loved one calling for her, telling her it will be okay.

She's falling and it hurts, but not because she's falling, and she knows it's the end.

She's falling and it hurts because no one cares if she falls anyway.

—

"Joy, come towards me, please." Joy hears the quake in Moira's voice, and it sends a note of fear down her spine.

Good. Fear is exactly what she needed to fly.

The waves crash into the rocky beach with incredible force. Unlike further north, this beach is known for its dangerous undertow, a challenge for swimmers and surfers alike on its calmest days—something today is not. Each wave reverberates up the shore, reaching near inches away from where Joy stands fully clothed, sneakers sinking into muddy rocks.

And yet, the wind whips at her face, hair, and clothes like she's already flying. A part of her wonders if it would carry her away before she could even get her bearings. But she's determined.

"It's going to be fine," Joy says as she turns to face her, wincing as Moira gasps. She can see the terror in her face at every inch Joy moves, and though Joy is angry at her, she doesn't envy Moira the horror she must be feeling.

"I've done this before. I tried to show you. You have to trust me. Watch!" Joy starts to turn, but a scream from Moira gives her pause. She turns her head back to see Moira has taken several steps towards her but has stopped short now that Joy has met her gaze.

Very real fear grips at Joy's chest, this time like a poison that sinks into her veins in sharp twinges. Moira's mascara is running down her cheeks in splotched tears, her face flushed red but her lips are pale.

"Stay there, Moira," she says, and she tries a smile this time.

It doesn't work. "Joy, we can talk about this safely at home. Let's go back to the car, get you to the therapist, to the people who can help you." She is pleading now, a tone Joy had never heard her use with anyone.

Joy grasps her arms in her hands, head lowering, curling in on herself, and shivering in sheer frustration. *Why can't she listen to me?*

Her voice is firm, even as her teeth chatter from the cold. "I know what I'm doing. I've made my decision. Why can't you trust me?"

Moira straightens, her face red as she wipes at her eyes, mascara streaking across her face. She lets out a bitter laugh that scratches at Joy's ears. "Trust you? This is crazy, Joy! You're insisting you can fly. What am I supposed to think?"

Joy feels the stinging at the corner of her eyes but presses on. Her mouth feels dry, but she works against it as she speaks. "You're supposed to listen to me! This could have been avoided if you'd listened to me in the first place! You're never with me, and when you're home it feels like you'd rather I not be there, like I'm the irritating noise in the room!"

Moira shakes her head as Joy finishes as if she can shake the words away. "This isn't about us, Joy, this is about your mental health and getting you help. And what did your therapist say about absolutes, Joy?"

She isn't going to listen. The thought should have sent her spiraling into despair but for the first time, Joy feels a sense of calm. *If she isn't going to listen, then I have nothing to gain, do I?*

Joy straightens, letting her arms fall to her sides, then lifts them slightly, palms facing forward. She raises her head towards the sky, letting the sun hit her face, and she lets out a laugh. *Maybe it's time to start with my own approval.*

"My therapist said there's no such things as absolutes. So then nothing is impossible." She looks at Moira, sees the sudden recognition, but it's too late.

"Joy, no." Moira takes a step forward—

Joy turns on her heel and runs towards the receding waves, her shoes smacking against the wet rocks and splashing water up behind her. Her feet just hit the edge of the water, her toes becoming soaked in the salty foam, when she jumps—

Maybe the difference between flying and falling is all about perspective.

—

The dream is always the same.

She's flying, and though the fear is like a leaden weight in her heart, it does not stop her.

There is no one to watch her fly, or fall, but she feels free.

FIREFLY SOUL

THEY ARE hard to spot at first. Our souls burn bright like fireflies, and the soulless are only the spaces between. Their absence is harder to impress against the background of stars in my vision.

I don't always see them. Souls. Or lack of souls, either. It's a gift that comes sporadically, usually after I experience some sort of low. It's like when you close your eyes after you look at a bright light; you can still see the glow behind your eyelids, but it fades.

When I was young, I resolved to never let the opportunity pass me by. I've renewed, as I call it, firefighters, paramedics, victims of abuse, people who witnessed out of order deaths, anything that causes seemingly irreversible trauma.

I can't heal them. But I can give them a path forward.

Today seems like it should be no different. Yet I see no empty space where a soul should be, no darkness in the hearts of any passers-by.

I'm tired. The weight is a mountain pressing down into my chest, a snare restricting my lungs. The reviving trigger, the thing that causes my sight to reappear, has been brutal. I am thankful for a chance to help someone, but my own soul feels heavy from my experience.

I move away from the wall where I've been holding myself steady along the sidewalk. I wasn't very aware of my surroundings when I leaned against the brick building, caught off guard by the sudden revival of my sight. Looking up at the sign, I see that it's a bookstore. I take it as a hint and walk through the doors, keeping my gaze soft and try to spot the black hole where a soul should be.

In this space it's easier to spot individuals than it was on the sidewalk, and I count it in my favor. But it's a large store, and my heartbeat slows at the seemingly endless rows of bookshelves. I feel drained, and the thought of going through row by row, even possibly missing someone on the other side of a bookshelf, of not finding the person I'm meant to help, all of it wears my resolve. I already see the edges of my sight dimming, and I know I'm running out of time.

I try not to look suspicious as I walk alongside the rows of bookshelves, looking down each individual row to see if I can spot my target. Fortunately, my search can be passed off as looking for a particular genre section, so there's no employee coming towards me in suspicion of shoplifting.

Try as I might, I find no missing souls from any of the patrons of the store. Tired, cranky, and at my breaking point, I return to the store entryway.

It's when my hand is hovering over the bar to open the glass door that I notice something strange. On the other side of the glass, there's a poster on dark paper. I hadn't seen my reflection coming in, but in the glass, contrasting the back of the black sheet of paper like a black mirror, I see myself. I see the empty place where my soul should be.

I bite back a sob and push the glass door open. I walk along the sidewalk and the several blocks until I get to my apartment, in a complete daze. Numb. The crowd around me passes in a blur of colors and light, my vision dimming but still strong enough for each light to burn the inside of my eyelids.

When I get to my apartment, I fumble with the keys, hands shaking. I drop my bag and kick off my shoes, all in a hurry before barging into the bathroom so I can see myself in the mirror over the sink.

The sight makes my breath catch in my throat. Where my soul should be is a black, sucking maw. Light bounces off and retracts, then the darkness encompasses it, leaving it blacker than the darkest black. It's a space where things don't die but live in stasis for an indeterminate amount of time.

How am I supposed to save myself?

I drop to the floor and lean my back against the side of the bathtub. I stretch out my legs below the sink, slouch against the tub, and rest my head on the porcelain lip.

I have no soul.

I wonder if I can pinpoint the moment when it happened. Oddly, I find that I can. It was the moment when she took her final breath, as if my soul left with hers.

My face is half numb, so I'm surprised to feel tears on my cheeks. I'm not sad per se; my emotions in a field of nothing, neither moving forward or backward. A liminal space between the life there was and the life I have now.

I know without checking the mirror that my sight has faded to nothing by the time I push myself up from the floor. I wonder how I'm supposed to know when my soul returns if there's no sight to see it with.

But somehow, I have a feeling I'll know.

It's not because I think I'll find joy, or happiness, or overcome the loss, make something of it, or any of the platitudes and well wishes I've heard at the funeral.

I'll know because to have a soul is to feel. To hurt.

I both want it and dread it.

As much as the numbness protects the heart that still beats in my chest, she doesn't deserve for our memories together to remain gray and dull. She deserves color.

I grab a tissue, wipe at my eyes, and inhale to the bottom of my lungs.

A soul is meant to hurt.

The trick is to survive it.

TRANSDIFFERENTIATE

DEAR EZRA HAYES,

At its meeting on March 12th, 2021, the Board of Trustees of The Pacific Marine Biology Foundation considered your request for $125,000 for the study of the Turritopsis Dohrnii in order to learn the viability of cell transdifferentiation in humans. However, the proposal was denied.

PMBF receives more requests than our limited resources can fund. This leads to difficult decisions in creating priorities and means that a number of important research projects cannot be supported by the foundation.

We are appreciative of the time and effort you put forth in preparing the application. Although the PMBF cannot be of assistance, we wish you success in acquiring the funds from other sources.

Sincerely,
Dr. Elizabeth J. Castenada
On a personal note, Ezra, please call me. This needs to stop.

—

Ezra watches dorsal fins bob in the distance, gliding over then below the surface of the choppy waves. The orange and yellow polygons of the sun reflect on the crests, seeming to whisk the pod of dolphins towards the horizon. The roaring light of the sun falls behind the waves at an indistinguishable pace, but the promise of night is imminent.

Jean would have waxed poetic about the beauty of the ocean. How it's our duty to learn as much as we can about it, that only twenty percent has been seen with human eyes. The thought sours his mood. Jean hasn't been on a trip with him in months. It's the whole reason he's here. No breathtaking sunset in the middle of the Pacific Ocean will distract him.

He moves about the boat with the grace of someone who finds more comfort in the constantly moving footing of the sea than the sturdiness of soil. He resumes getting his equipment together, his mission at the forefront of his mind.

Getting a sample of tissue from a *Turritopsis Dohrnii* is proving to be an arduous, despair-inducing task. The thrill of achieving scientific success is usually enough to keep him focused and patient with the necessary number of failed attempts to secure samples of even one of his toughest prey—jellyfish. Today, his fingers shake as his mind stutters on memories of antiseptic and beeping monitors.

I can't afford another wasted trip. Every time I go back to shore empty-handed may be the last.

It takes longer than he likes to ready the metal and glass pods used to capture specimens along with the equipment he needs to process and preserve samples. The sun has already set by the time he's ready. The boat's floodlights make the ocean seem like a dark abyss past his reach, beyond recognition from the crisp blue waves and marshmallow clouds from the afternoon.

Solo trips this far into the Pacific are a suicide mission, one he's successfully completed several times on his own. So much could go wrong. It doesn't help that Ezra purposely neglects to inform the U.S. Coast Guard or any of his colleagues of his whereabouts. No one even knows he left.

Not that I have anyone who'd risk their lives or equipment to help me at this point. I'm lucky to even still have this boat.

Eleven trips and no success. In the early days of his research, he'd barely made two trips before he had enough samples of jellyfish gastrodermis to not have to go out again for weeks. Now that he's so close to the culmination of his research, the sparseness of sightings and empty pods are wearing him down.

He pushes the thoughts away, attempting to focus on forcing his shaking hands to place the bait in one of the pods. He then lowers it over the edge of the boat. The chain cranks out at a measured pace to ensure proper depth. When fully lowered, he connects the buoy before he moves on to the next spot.

Each buoy disappears behind the boat into complete blackness as if swallowed, and Ezra silently thanks Jean for installing a more updated GPS for charting coordinates before … well. Before.

After six more pods are placed, Ezra moves the boat further away from the last buoy, not wanting to risk the proximity to the final pod affecting his results.

He sets out the anchor and cuts the engine. He shuts off the floodlights, keeping a small clamp light near the main console. Work complete, he retreats towards the back of the boat where a chair and a woolen blanket are set up.

All that's left to do is wait. Wait, and hope, I guess.

Knowing sleep will elude him, Ezra wraps himself in the thread-bare blanket and lets his head fall back on the chair. His eyes swim through the stars, his view slowly rocking in the dizzying sway of the ocean's surface as he tries to name the constellations Jean taught him.

—

A successful trip and several priceless samples locked away in temperature and moisture regulated containers are enough to lift Ezra's spirits into some semblance of awareness. It has been weeks of fitful nights and an unhealthy amount of black coffee.

The mood doesn't last.

The hospital called as soon as he'd set his equipment inside his home. He assumes they're going to discuss Jean's recent test results, and he feels the fear like swallowed nails in his gut.

He makes it to the hospital within the hour, bringing with him another book of crosswords for Jean and a book for himself. That Jean doesn't look any worse than the last time he'd been there gives him a bit of hope, but by the time the doctor makes it to Jean's room he's had enough hours to gnaw down his thumbnails.

The news is grim.

"I'm sorry, but the latest scan indicates that surgery is no longer a viable solution. The chemo and radiation therapy did buy us more time; however, the cancer has progressed further than we had hoped at this point. We cannot remove the tumors without causing irreversible brain damage. I would recommend continued chemotherapy to prolong for a few weeks, but there is nothing more we can do."

Jean watches the doctor explain with hooded eyes. The acceptance and apathy in them make Ezra want to vomit, throw something, rage at the doctor, and demand more testing.

Say something, do something, there has to be a solution. Please, don't give up.

Seemingly unaware of Ezra's internal struggle, Jean nods, tight-lipped but clearly not at all angry at either the doctor or the news.

"I see," Jean comments calmly as if viewing unfavorable results from an exploratory study. "I … thought as much, to be honest. Thank you for everything you've done."

And Jean, sweet naive Jean, holds his hand towards the doctor as if he were receiving a rejection on a funding proposal instead of a death sentence. His once firm handshake is frail and jerky as he shakes the doctor's hand, inclining his head slightly.

Dismissed, the doctor stands from his seat, gathers his clipboard and folder, and makes his way towards the door in his pristine white coat and black leather dress shoes.

Don't just shake his hand, Ezra implores Jean with his gaze. *Don't give up. You can't. This can't be it. I need more time.*

He stands sharply but is startled as Jean's right hand grabs at his forearm, his grip stronger than the handshake he'd witnessed.

"Stop," Jean says, tone unflinching, "Stop, Ezra. Don't make things worse."

Ezra stares at Jean's pale, gaunt face. Jean's eyes, once sharp and analyzing, are now murky and dull from the chemotherapy. They stare forward as if the walls of the hospital room are the only thing in the world worth studying anymore. Even though Ezra is certain he knows the sight well enough to draw a diagram without looking.

"Make things worse?" Ezra says, barely processing Jean's words. "How could things be worse? Jean, he told you he's giving up on you. They're not even going to try anymore. They're going to let you die. How can I make that worse than what it is?"

Jean closes his glacier-colored eyes, and Ezra pushes down his relief at not having to see them so lifeless. He doesn't want to remember Jean's eyes any other way than the ones he stared into during their wedding vows.

He's determined to see them like that again.

"It can't be a surprise to you, Ezra. We're both scientists. We knew it was a long shot the moment I was diagnosed. What was it Maddie always said? Numbers don't lie; don't be mad at their honesty. They really don't give a fuck."

Ezra shakes his head fitfully. Maddie had said that on many occasions. None of those occasions had meant the death of the love of his life, though.

"So that's it? You're going to give up, let cancer win?"

Jean opens his eyes, turning towards Ezra. His gaze is cold, purple rings like permanent bruises below his bottom lids. Ezra has never seen Jean so tired in his life. Not even when they'd both suffered through grad school and doctorate courses while working two jobs.

"Is that what you think? That this is some life-threatening game that I'm choosing to give up on because I don't have the will to make it to the finish line? Don't be stupid, Ezra. This isn't a problem you can solve or a test you can study for or retake. We tried, we failed, it's done. I don't want to spend what time I have moaning about what little there is left of it."

Ezra feels like all his bones have been removed at once, yet still hears his knees cracking at the suddenness of him sitting in the creaky folding chair.

"Jean, please," is all he can manage to say, voice weak as if his vocal cords are locked tight.

Jean shakily grasps Ezra's hand and pulls it onto the edge of the bed over the covers to save energy. Ezra stares at their clasped hands, wondering when his husband's bones became visible on the surface.

"Ezra," Jean starts. He pauses. He inhales slowly, and Ezra can hear the shakiness of his lungs in that breath. "There are some things we need to talk about beforehand. I know you're upset; I know you're angry. You can't think I'm not too."

Ezra can't lift his gaze. Can't watch that mouth he'd kissed so often form these words. He watches as Jean gives his little remaining energy to trace circles on the back of Ezra's hand.

"But if we don't talk about it, it will make later on so much harder for you. Please, I can't be the cause of that. I love you. You know I do. I will fight to stay with you as long as I can, I promise. But you need to fight too. You need to fight to stay with me too."

Ezra lifts his chin slightly, eyes searching for Jean's.

"Doing this to you is my biggest regret. We said till death do us part, and I guess I never thought of the parting portion of that. That one of us would be left behind. For that, I'm sorry. I don't regret marrying you, never, but I'm so, so sorry Ezra. I wanted to see you finish your research, see you bald and get laugh lines and wrinkles."

Jean pauses with a wet inhale. His hand squeezes Ezra's briefly, clearly holding back emotion and fear.

"I wanted to grow old with you."

I'm making this harder on him. I can't let him despair. I can't break him more before I fix him.

"Okay," Ezra finally says. "Okay. I guess we have some plans to make."

———

The syringe is surprisingly unremarkable and easy to sneak through hospital security.

It contains a world-changing concoction of genetically modified cells that would render humanity biologically immortal, packed away with care in the inner pocket of his jacket.

It isn't until he is yards away from Jean's hospital room door that his excitement gives way to an unfortunate flaw in his plan.

Getting the injection to Jean isn't the issue. Human trials are inherently different from animal trials, and as confident as Ezra is in his serum, testing his first formula on the love of his life is out of the question.

But so are human trials. He no longer has the funding or reputation to even approach a research team. His obsession with finding a cure for Jean's cancer led to cutting ties with all those relationships, even the ones he most cherished.

At first, it had been arguments and petty disagreements. Ostentatious ridicule of his theories and well-meaning interventions to keep him focused on his real work, to keep living even though his partner was dying. As if the rest of the world simply kept rotating on its axis, but Ezra's was tilted towards ruin.

He couldn't deny that the final cuts had been all him. There was anger after he'd been forced to scavenge much-needed supplies from the laboratories of colleagues. It was only the last vestiges of their friendship that stopped Liz and so many others from pressing charges.

On top of that, none of his research had been sanctioned, so it would have to be redone. Ethics committee would never even let him go near a trial for the lack of ethical considerations from the start. Even if they were able to find the funding or resources, it would take a monumental amount of time—far more than the days or weeks they had. The actual trials would take time, too. Going from rat to human would take years, plus the difference in mass alone ... There were so many variables and so many ways it could veer off-course.

He didn't have that time.

It didn't take long after Jean's devastating test results for his condition to decline. Despite Ezra's protests, he was refusing further treatment, wanting to spend the rest of his time with Ezra free from the effects of chemotherapy.

The first week had been manageable, spending time holding each other, Ezra reading aloud to Jean—who could no longer focus on the printed word—and listening to albums from their youth on Ezra's phone.

After nine days, Jean didn't recognize him. While that first episode hadn't lasted, they became more frequent.

He is out of time.

Out of time and out of options. Ezra's fingers rub the bridge of his nose habitually. *But I can't inject Jean with an untested formula. I can put my ethics aside, but my heart just can't do it. It could kill him quicker than the cancer.*

He leans against the wall across from Jean's doorway, eyes unfocused and half-lidded, something he did when he wanted to absorb himself in his thoughts without too much visual stimulation. His "problem-solving face", Jean had called it.

He is running through the composition of the formula and effects on the rats he'd tested on when he faintly hears the voice of Jean's doctor. Looking around, he realizes the door for the room across the hallway from Jean's is half-open. Inside he can hear Jean's doctor speaking to another patient.

"We'll continue with chemotherapy and radiation. The tumors have progressed quite quickly, but we'll be doing everything we can to prevent it from metastasizing so we can perform the surgery."

Ezra strains to hear the doctor's words even as his chest constricts, hands trembling at the plan forming in the back of his mind.

———

The child is no more than eight. The monitors beep like a metronome, a steady rhythm that belies the sight of the weak and broken boy lying on the rough sheets of the hospital bed. His face is pale, lips ghostly, bruised eyes the only contrast to the white of the pillowcase.

It figures it would be a child. Ezra knows that even if the child recovers from the cancer because of his formula, following through with this plan will break something in him that can never be repaired.

No matter what happens moving forward, he can never breathe a word to Jean for fear of the horror in his face.

This is crazy. He clenches his teeth, hoping to squeeze the thoughts of terror and self-loathing out of his head. *This can't possibly work. This formula is for a body twice this kid's size, to begin with, ignoring all the other uncountable factors I haven't calculated for.*

He isn't going to do it.

He isn't going to.

He won't.

He remembers Jean's eyes, the bottomless pools of their wedding day. The murky, infected, frothy waters they are today.

I have no other choice. Sorry, kid. Either you become a part of history today or your story ends here.

In retrospect, it is far too easy. He waits until the end of visitor hours, the child's family slow to leave and every second they dawdle leaves another crescent shaped mark on Ezra's palms from his nails digging in. When they leave, he makes his move.

Now, his body moves disconnected from a mind that refuses to face the choice he's made.

He silently makes his way towards the IV drip, uncapping the syringe with minimal noise. He gently picks up the medical tubing between his thumb and forefinger, setting the needle next to the plastic tubing and bracing himself for whatever comes.

The needle pierces the tube in a short, fluid motion. He presses the plunger down slowly, allowing the clear formula to slowly mix with the saline a bit at a time, hoping the slow injection will allow the boy's body time to adjust.

As the dosage tapers off, Ezra's gaze flickers toward where the boy lies still. He pulls his eyes back quickly, not able to handle watching the face of the boy he may be poisoning. He removes the needle and carefully places the syringe into a small acrylic tube.

Better to not leave this here as evidence. I'll keep it on me until I get to my workshop.

He carefully releases the medical tubing, shuffling back away from the IV and the hospital bed, careful not to rustle any of the other equipment as he retreats.

I should know within minutes, Ezra considers. The process of reverting the cells back to their initial stage will take time, but whether his body is able to absorb it … that won't take long.

The previously continuous rhythm of the boy's heart rate mon itor suddenly staggers, then starts to flutter quickly, warning beeps sounding. Ezra has no time to process his mistake.

Keeping his pace steady and purposeful, gaze at his feet, he leaves.

—

He failed. He failed, and someone—no, not just someone, a child—died because of it.

Ezra's mind spirals. There is no time to create a new formula. The only possibility he can actually take action on is that the dosage was too strong for the small, frail body.

It's something. Hope is fading, but some part of Ezra still clings to it. *I have one dose left.*

The call from earlier had been grim. There was a very real possibility that this trip will be the last time he'll see Jean alive.

Ezra grabs an overstuffed duffel bag and fills it with anything he thinks he could possibly need for the last night with his husband. He wedges the syringe in an inconspicuous side pocket.

Even if I don't go through with it, well, better to have it just in case.

—

Ezra swears he can smell the life dripping out of Jean's pores in his cold sweat. It permeates the air and lays thick like an invisible toxic gas in the room, odorless and yet ripe like crumbling bones to the touch. As if even his senses are confused and backward with the impossibility of what is happening.

They play whatever simple card game they can that requires little movement or sight on Jean's part—which turns out to be a somewhat stilted yet intimate game of Go Fish. Ezra carefully ignores when Jean mistakes one card for another even as he holds it inches from his face.

Little white lies.

When that becomes too much, Ezra makes up stories about the progress of his research. Faces they have in common come and go as he spins his tales, even making up new characters that flit in and out of the stories. Jean smiles softly, chuckles lightly even in his weak state, makes the appropriate frowns, and slight shakes of his head where appropriate.

More lies, but not the worst he's perpetrated in recent months.

When Jean starts to have trouble following the stories, Ezra pulls out the portable turntable and sets it up to play softly near Jean's bedside. Pulling out an LP of The Clash from Jean's teenage years, he drops the needle onto the record and settles his chair close enough to Jean to hold his hand as Jean's head lies back, eyes closed.

Ezra studies Jean's face as he dozes. His Jean. Nothing at all like the quietly confident man with a slightly hunched posture and day-old stubble he'd loved for so many years. The bulky glasses are gone, his barely-there eyebrows the only hair that managed any sort of regrowth after stopping chemo.

This is not the Jean he married. This Jean is his husband, the one he would sacrifice all he's earned and everything he hadn't in order to save.

"I talked to Liz, you know. And Ivan."

The words are slow, stuttered. They catch Ezra by surprise, his brain momentarily disconnecting from his mouth long enough for Jean to continue.

"Ivan said you haven't been focusing on your research for months. Since I was admitted. That you lost your funding and your license and are in danger of losing your boat too. And our home."

Ezra's blood becomes sludge, hypothermic before, like a jet-stream, it starts to flow quickly through his heart.

"Liz said you stole from her. And Michael, too."

Jean's eyes are still closed. He is even paler than before like his skin could go translucent at any moment.

"Ezra. I don't … you have to tell me. Explain it to me."

Suddenly, the toxicity in the air burns down his throat, the thoughts of 'I can't let him die like this' and 'now he knows what a monster I am,' and 'please not now' filling his skull.

"I can't let you die." The words are out of his mouth before he can pull them back. They're like a lighter in a room of noxious fumes.

Jeans' eyes open. They are murky with pain. Ezra can see the sadness and bone-deep acceptance in them. He hasn't seen that same pain since Jean's sister cut herself out of his life—when she finally understood that Ezra wasn't going anywhere.

Jean turns his head slightly towards him, and Ezra inches off the chair to lean over Jean's form so he can stay put.

"It isn't up to you, Ezra. It's not up to me either."

A pause, Jean inhaling slowly. His eyes are wet, but his body can't do more than that in this state. The cancer won't even let him cry.

"Let me go, Ezra. Please. Don't make me the reason you fail what we tried so hard to complete. I've fought so hard. Please. I need you to let me go. I need you to fight too. Don't let me die thinking I've destroyed you."

When Ezra's fingers trace Jean's cheek, locking eyes with his husband's, he sheds tears for both of them.

"Okay," Ezra says. "Okay. I'll finish what we started Jean. I won't stop fighting."

Ezra crawls onto the flimsy hospital mattress and holds his husband in his arms for two more hours. At 2:51 am, the last coherent words Ezra ever hears from his husband is asking him to turn off the monitors.

The nurse stops in to check on them, and Ezra quietly informs her that they would like some peace for the last bit of his husband's life.

At 4:47 am, Ezra stops his slow stroking of Jean's hand lying between them.

Carefully removing himself from the grasp of his husband, he quietly walks over to the duffel bag. The syringe makes no noise as he pulls it from the hidden pocket.

———

James bangs his hand one more time against the clear acrylic of the vending machine before his forehead follows suit with a slightly gentler thud.

That was my last dollar bill. Fuck. This.

"You might as well try the slots instead," Miranda snickers. "You'd have about the same amount of luck."

James peels himself off the machine in defeat. He pads over to the table, and his muscles and bones drain into the creaky plastic chair next to her like molasses. He lets his head hit the table—gently this time—and pulls his arms up to rest over the back of his head.

"I'd probably have better luck with the slots, but I'm pretty fucking sure they aren't allowed in hospitals, so I'm really shit out of luck."

Miranda pats his shoulder lightly. Hearing a crinkling, James looks up to see her sliding a bag of baked potato chips his way.

He knew she was his favorite resident for a reason.

"So what's it this time?" Her question is to the point, and he puzzles on the best way to respond as he tries to open the metallic bag without the blessed food flying everywhere.

"There's an investigation, actually. Both the hospital, and the police. All asking the same goddamn questions."

Miranda doesn't seem to be able to decide whether he is being facetious, but soldiers on anyway. "About what? You work with the almost-always-terminal cancer patients, right? Who's gonna murder them or whatever?"

James shrugs, finally getting the bag open. "It's kind of the opposite, actually. Some really freaky things going on at our floor."

Miranda grabs the bag out of James' hands, holding it up and to her other side. "How can you do the opposite of murder? That makes no sense. And this is a bribe, not a free lunch. Welcome to America."

James rolls his eyes, halfheartedly swiping for the bag out of his reach. He's secretly glad to relay what little he's gleaned from the chaos sweeping through his ward. "You know, I was born and raised in America. You came from London or whatever. I'm pretty sure that should be the other way around, but fine."

James leans back in his chair, valiantly trying to rearrange his spine back to its original, healthy position but giving up as he always does after a few loud creaks.

"First it was this kid. The fairly typical case—diagnosed stage four, goes through chemo and radiation, is looking like he'll be a good candidate for surgery but then he suddenly flat lines one night. They pronounce him dead, the parents see him, they send for the coroner."

Miranda pulls a single chip out of the bag now, waving it near his nose, like the aroma would entice him more. As if a small bag of stale chips smells like anything but mothballs.

"And?" She sounds impatient yet still curious.

"When the coroner comes up to take him to the morgue, the kid's sitting up and asking about his Nintendo DS. Thinks he's had his tonsils removed or something. Scared the shit out of her."

The chip pauses mid-flight, Miranda temporarily stunned enough for him to grab at it. He only manages to crack it apart, crumbs hitting the table. "Wait. He survived? How the fuck did they think he was dead?"

James waves his hand in dismissal. "Dunno. They thought they'd made a mistake. Damn, were his parents pissed. Started yelling about suing the hospital, wanted the doctor's medical license taken away, the works."

Miranda leans back, still facing James. She sets the bag of chips on the table, uninterested in teasing anymore. "Well, that's unusual and pretty screwed up, but not unheard of."

James snatches the bag before Miranda can change her mind.

"That's not the craziest part, though. They move him to a different hospital right after that. Start him back on chemo and radiation. He seemed to be improving, super fast too. But when they did a CAT scan to evaluate him for surgery, there's nothing. The tumors, cancer, everything is gone."

Miranda stares at him. He had her hooked. "Gone. As in … what?"

James slowly opens his mouth, placing a chip on his tongue before chewing slowly. Payback.

"G-O-N-E. Like he hadn't had cancer at all. All the cancerous cells were gone, and there were new, absolutely normal brain cells in their place. Took part of his memory though, he didn't remember the past few years at all."

Miranda shakes her head slightly, clearly trying to find a reason behind what sounded like an urban legend. "Wait, so, did he never have it then? They're suing the hospital, so was it malpractice?"

James shrugs, stuffing another few chips into his mouth before continuing.

"Nope. The hospital he'd transferred to scanned him when he first came, to be sure. It was there when he got there. Then gone in a few weeks. The hospital tried to claim it was their doing, but, well, then something similar happened to another patient here."

James pauses to shake the crumbs from the mostly empty bag into his mouth, then starts speaking again while he searches the table for his bottle of water.

"This patient—some sort of scientist or something—he was pretty much on his last few hours. Terminal, nothing we could do. The nurse said his husband was staying with him that last night so they left them alone. In the morning when they switched shifts, the nurse hadn't realized why the room was shut off so she checked in on them. The husband was gone, but the patient was sitting up in bed, not at all dead and hardly dying either."

Miranda continues shaking her head. James doesn't blame her. Shaking a new world view into place seemed as good a technique as any. "And the husband? When was this? Why the police?"

"The husband is why the police are here, actually. It seems either he or someone who wanted him dead torched his house, his boat, his car, everything. No one's seen him since that night."

Miranda rubs at her eyes. "That's horrible, honestly. You cheat death and wake up to your husband dead or at least missing."

James shrugs. "Can't be too upset about it. He remembers absolutely nothing. He's basically a blank slate, complete amnesia. They're even working on helping him remember to read and write. He somehow remembers random shit like the family and classes of random sea life but not the alphabet. You know how the brain is—however the new cells got there, they destroyed the old. Brains are strange things sometimes."

Miranda attempts to hide a small smile. Completely inappropriate, but you didn't get far in the medical field without a slightly macabre sense of humor.

"Alright, you got me beat. That is officially the weirdest hospital war story I've heard so far. Go ahead, keep wasting your bottom dollar in the vending machines as you wish. I won't stop ya. Luck is about as good a thing to put your faith in as anything at this point."

James pauses after standing, a thought flitting in the periphery of his skull. "It's a habit at this point. Deal with shit the same way long enough, it doesn't even occur to you to try something else until it's too late."

He grabs the empty chip bag, throwing it towards the trash bin, winces as it missed.

Sighing, he takes the seven steps towards the failed attempt at a free throw, bends down to grab the bag, and throws it into the trash can properly.

"Guess there's always tomorrow."

—

Transdifferentiation, also known as lineage reprogramming, is a process in which one mature somatic cell transforms into another mature somatic cell ... There are no known instances where adult cells change directly from one lineage to another except Turritopsis Dohrnii and in the Turritopsis Nutricula, a jellyfish that is theoretically immortal.
   -Wikipedia

SLEEPING DOGS DON'T LIE

THE BITING AIR prickles the skin on his face. Caleb saves his hands by burying them in his coat pockets, but the cold still penetrates down to his bones.

It is a terrible start to his new job. Possibly soon to be his old job if things don't change. His boss took him aside at the end of the day to warn him of his poor performance — as if he hadn't known himself.

Walking towards his subsidized apartment along the deserted street, it takes all his willpower to keep the damning thoughts at bay. He's messed up, and now the best he can hope for is a minimum wage job serving white middle-class accountants and doctors their morning coffee. It is a dead-end, and he knows it.

Maybe it is better to give up now.

Rounding the corner, he jumps as a dark shape runs towards him, his mind only retroactively registering that it is behind a metal fence. The shape, a black and white, hulking pitbull, stops at the edge and stands up on his hind legs to try to reach him, his whole lower half shaking with his tail. He is panting with joy in his eyes as if he has been waiting for Caleb.

With a worn smile, Caleb reaches his arm forward to let the dog sniff at his fingers. Its mouth closes and head tilts as he — she? — does just that. Once the dog is satisfied that he is an acceptable companion, it bumps its nose into his hand, demanding pets.

Caleb's smile becomes warm as he scratches behind the dog's ears. He twists the collar around to read the name on the metal tag: Daisy.

"Hello, Daisy," he says, "It's nice to meet you. You have such a beautiful smile, sweet girl." She leans into the touch and licks his hand in return.

And if he enters his apartment with a smile, no one else will ever know.

—

His visits to Daisy on his long trek home became routine. By summer, she waits for him like clockwork at the fence. In turn he brings her dog biscuits, toys, and bits of rope they play tug of war with.

Work gets better. Everything gets better. By fall he has a job offer one town over that promises paid time off and benefits. He is being given a second chance, and while he is overjoyed now that his future is only getting brighter, there is another bright spot in his life that he will miss.

The day the moving truck is loaded, he knows it is time to say goodbye. He has bought a large box of peanut butter cookies meant for dogs from a local bakery, complete with a red bow on top and a card. It may have been overboard for someone who won't understand the gesture, but Daisy meant more to him than she would ever understand anyway.

Except Daisy isn't in the yard. It isn't unusual—he rarely ever sees her this time of day so he shouldn't have been surprised. But that doesn't move the lump forming in his throat.

Making an impulsive decision, he decides that if Daisy can't come to him, he'll go to her. He rounds the corner to the building that is connected to the gated yard. It is an attached brick home, two stories with the black metal gate along the side. It isn't cheap, even for that area, but he is filled with an overwhelming need to see his rescuer before he leaves.

Gathering his courage, he walks up the concrete steps and knocks firmly on the door. He hears noises coming from the other side, and after what feels like minutes a stocky, white-haired older woman wearing a soft gray knit sweater opens the door.

"Can I help you?" she asks, her voice congenial but confused.

He flounders for a few seconds before he offers her the box. "I live in the apartment a few blocks down, but I'm moving away. I wanted to give these to your dog, as a thank you."

The woman shakes her head, mouth thinning. "I don't have a dog. You must be mistaking this house with another."

Caleb furrows his brow, mouth gaping at the unexpected answer. It is a strange request he is making, sure, but this is unexpected.

"Daisy isn't your dog? Then who's dog is she?"

The woman's eyes widen, and she brings her wrinkled hand to her chest. She inhales with a start, tilts her head in question. "Daisy? Whenever did you see Daisy?"

Caleb lowers the box of biscuits, his heart pounding with fear. Did something happen to his Daisy? "I saw her yesterday, in the yard."

She inhales sharply and her eyes widen.

"I'm sorry, you must be mistaken." The lady wipes at her eyes and shakes her head with mouth quaking. "She's been gone a long time now. My dear Daisy died four years ago."

AS FOR THE BEES

THE BEEKEEPER CAN TASTE the despair in the honey.

It isn't only that there is less of it, or that most of his hives have collapsed. Rather, the sticky, sugary syrup tastes less sweet and more like a bitter despondence. Like even his bees have given up hope.

———

She has meddled with the order of things she doesn't understand. A wish has become a maelstrom, and she doesn't know how to stop it.

———

"We've been out for weeks; manufacturing's at a standstill. If we don't get more, we're going to have to change our formula. We can't afford that. They'll shut the business down for good." He wipes the sweat from his brow and lowers his face mask to breathe inside the stuffy, sweltering building. There is a moment of static, the noise a stark contrast to the echoing bangs from when the machines still ran.

"I don't know what to tell ya. It's like the damned bees flew off to hell knows where. There's nothing there, man. No one's got it."

—

Perhaps it isn't too late, time a fluctuating thing that she can mend, mold like a waterway into a dam. If only she is careful.

—

Dead. Dead. Drying. Dead. No fruit. No seeds. A yellowed, decaying acre, twisting winds blowing up dirt and debris along with the sharp scent of decay.

"Another one, gone," he says, though his wife is too far away to hear his voice in the wind. He drops the rough, dried plant from his hands, and it falls like vertigo that resounds in a closing door.

—

In her haste, they have gotten away from her, hummed a gentle tenor around her ears, and ducked into paned windows, hoping to release themselves from their glass and wooden prison.

—

"It's the bees," he says. "Or rather, the lack of them."
He pushes the carefully crafted folder towards his supervisor,

overfull with a stack of papers from his immersive study. It has taken months of testing, cataloging, and monitoring populations. The results aren't unexpected but carry the weight of a judge's mallet.

His supervisor doesn't open the folder. Instead, he taps an uneven rhythm on the desk with his fingers.

"And you expect us to do, what?"

The question catches him off guard. "You didn't ask me to figure out a solution, just to find the problem."

His supervisor leans forward on his elbows, bringing his face close to his own. "The economy is collapsing. Shortages of food and consumer goods across the globe. Manufacturing is shutting down. You brought me the problem. Now tell me how to fix it."

He gulps in precious air, knowing it isn't the answer he wants to hear.

"We can't."

—

She'd been innocent in her intentions, but that doesn't stop the wave that overcomes the world. Robert Frost was wrong, she thinks, before she takes the plunge into darkness.

The world doesn't end in fire or ice.

It ends with bees and regrets.

FIRE STARTER

HEATED LIMBS REACH and spark from the burning logs and hot coals, fingers playing patterns against the darkness. Lena watches them from hooded eyes, lashes low across her view as she lets the sight of the eyes, the bodies, the anguished faces in the flames blur into each other. She pulls the thick sherpa blanket tighter around her neck with one hand and tightens her grip on Ivory's waist with the other.

"What you thinking?" Ivory asks, voice quiet and muffled against the crook of Lena's neck. It sounds loud, almost sacrilegious to disturb the near silence of the campsite this late at night. There are only the scattered remains of campfires and the sound of crickets breaking the constellation of stars above and darkness below. And

Ivory as she nestles into Lena's side. Lena swallows against the feeling of bile rising in her throat at the trust she's being given. She expects an answer.

"About you," she says, though the lie sounds flat even to her own ears. Lena feels the smile against her skin, and Ivory slaps her stomach before burrowing deeper into her, twisting an arm under Lena's shirt to encircle her curved waist.

"Lies," Ivory says through a laugh as she settles. "But sweet lies. What are you really thinking?"

Lena focuses on her breathing, closing her eyes to the flames, even as the light dances through her eyelids. *There has never been any running away from this, has there?*

"I'm thinking of a different fire from a different time," Lena finally answers. She leans deeper back onto the rock they claimed, pulling Ivory with her.

"Oh? Is this part of your epic back story that you never tell me about?"

Lena hums as she leans her head onto Ivory's. Her tone was light, but there is still an edge of annoyance and fear to the words. They'd argued over Lena's inability to share her history, true, but Lena is always shocked when she hears the fear. *As if I could ever leave her. She's the best thing to ever happen to me.*

"You could say that," Lena says. She untangles Ivory's hand from her waist and takes the fingers in her gloved hand, tracing the knuckles, the nails. "It's nothing I like to talk about. But you should know."

Quiet. Then cold air as Ivory unravels from her side. There's an apology on her tongue, but Ivory is there again, arms around her waist, face to face this time.

"Tell me." The words aren't demanding but pleading. Ivory's green eyes search Lena's own brown eyes, freckled by the oranges and yellows of the fire light. There's a warmth that has nothing to do with the fire that starts at Lena's fingertips and ends in her chest, blossoms like a raging storm. *Please don't let this be what makes you leave.*

"I'll tell you," she answers after a moment, then licks her lips. Her mouth feels dry, and the words don't want to form. "As long as you promise me something first."

Ivory runs her hands up and down Lena's arms, sending goosebumps along the flesh, not blinking from her gaze. "Anything."

"Promise you'll never ask me to call upon it."

—

Lena eyes the flames with what little self-preservation a six-year-old can muster—enough to keep her vinyl-lined jacket away from the reaching sparks and twisting smoke.

Her excitement has dimmed since the words 'campfire' transformed from theory into practice. She wants the experience of her classmates. The smores, the scary stories, the starlit sky. But she's never been so close to fire in her life.

Now she stares at the dancing flames with a wide-mouthed expression, her curiosity a tangible thing between her gulping breaths. She kneels in front of the fire, the stick and marshmallow she'd begged for forgotten.

"Are you going to cook your marshmallow or stare?" her mother calls out in amusement from behind her, sitting back in her folding chair. Lena doesn't switch her gaze from the swirling miasma of flames.

"How do they do that?" Lena asks and points towards the fire with her chubby fingers peeking through the overly large jacket sleeves.

The conversation around the fire dims, except for a creak as Lena's mother leans into her space and places a gentle hand on her shoulder.

"Who does what?" she whispers.

"The people in the fire," Lena replies. "How do they not burn?"

There's a curse behind her, and Lena turns in time to see her father's chair crash back from the force of him standing, his form retreating into the shadows towards the house. She can't make out most of the words beyond the odd swear and "hexerei."

Her fingers shake, and she inches away from the flames, which feel frigid and painful on her skin. When she looks at her mother's face, a cold fog of breath escapes between barely opened lips as she stares at Lena in horror.

"Dochder, no. Not you too."

—

The faces, the hands, the eyes in the flames are always there after that. Candles, the flame on their gas-lit stove, and of course, the rare campfire are all host to whatever spirits can't move on.

It's the gift of the matriarchs of the Kohler family. Her grandmother shares the gift, but it skipped her mother. When she returns that night, her grandmother promises to tell her of all the stories the flames tell her, of the nights spent communing with those who dance in the flames. She looks at Lena with pride, eyes crinkling to near slits as she speaks of how she will teach Lena the ways of the Fire Starter.

The following morning, she comes down for breakfast, excited to speak with her grandmother, only to find her sullen and despondent. One look at her parents tells her everything she needs to know.

Her father calls it a curse. Her mother watches her with thinly veiled fear.

She learns to ignore the visions, the goosebumps whenever she is around a fire, the feeling of being called to the flames, that she is forgetting to do something important. She finds fire no longer gives off warmth to her cupped hands. Most days her fingers feel cold and achy, like she will never be warm again. She takes to wearing gloves around the house to her mother's consternation, but when she asks, she only avoids her gaze.

"Come to the fire," her mother asks one autumn night, as if she doesn't remember her daughter's penchant for seeing dancing spirits in the flames. As if that is something easily forgotten. "You can warm yourself here and take off those gloves. They should be washed."

Now at eight, Lena likes to think herself grown up enough to sense danger coming when she sees it. She shakes her head and stuffs her hands beneath her armpits where her chair is turned away from the fire. The sight always leaves an aching in her chest she doesn't understand.

She hears a sigh from behind her, then the creaking of a folding chair. Too late, Lena tries to stand, but her mother with a surprising show of strength turns the chair she's sitting in around to face the fire and grabs hold of both Lena's arms. Her mother plucks a thick glove from Lena's hand, and grasps at her fingers with hands heated by the fire. They feel overwarm and clammy against Lena's, but glorious. She revels in it.

"Ach du lieva," she gasps, "your hands are freezing! Come to the fire; you'll catch your death."

Lena stiffens and pulls her hand back and reaches for her glove, but her mother is quicker. "Give it back, Mudder," she whines. "I want to go inside."

Instead, her mother grabs for her other hand and takes that glove too, putting them both in her apron pocket and pulling Lena up by the arm. "None of that, Lena. This is time for family. You always avoid the fire; it's time you sat with us instead of pouting in the corner. Come. Warm up."

Lena digs in her heels, but her mother is stronger than her and determined. She drags Lena and the rickety chair closer to the fire with little trouble. She settles the chair next to her own before plopping Lena into it.

Her mother gives her a hug around the shoulders and kisses her on the forehead, but all Lena sees is the swirling faces, arms, and hands of the spirits in the blaze as they reach for her. While once they had been dancing, now they're tormented and anguished, their faces elongating in the flames into silent screams, fingers splayed and gnarled.

Lena shivers and tucks her arms under legs, hoping to scavenge what little warmth she can. Wind emanates from the fire, a breeze that smells of burning plastic, acrid and unnatural.

Above the flames, barely visible through the waving air and scattered smoke rising from it, Lena spies her grandmother, wispy-white, straggled hair thin and falling from its braid, staring under wrinkled eyelids into the flames, curled into a thick knitted throw. Despite the suffocating heat from the fire, does she also feel the cold pinpricks down to her bones? The disconnection from the fire a longing that permeates each cell?

She feels the unfairness like a cold sweat that slicks down her cheeks and pools at the crook of her collarbone. When she looks back at the fire, in a surge of revolt, she locks eyes with one of the aching souls smoldering in the flames. It whirls in the colors that burn mirror images below her eyelids when she blinks. But she doesn't turn away. The longer she looks, the eyes become softer, less jagged, less terrorized. Eyelids form, then a differentiation between the pupil and iris, and then she can see defined eyelashes.

Sounds, unrecognizable as a word but repetitive, echo in her mind, and Lena chases it as the eyes fill her vision. She follows the pathways through a labyrinth, the name—because that's what it was—one step ahead, until all at once, she reaches the center.

Eliza.

That was her name. Eliza.

As if summoned, memories like photographs appear in her mind, scattered and jumbled beyond making any sense, and Lena's breath quickens at the overload. There's two children, a brother and sister; and then the brother is gone; a funeral for her brother, *how can she go on*? Then the brother is there again, but this time she stands in front of him, in front of their father, her mother crying, holding her brother's urn; he will pay; *fire, fire everywhere*—

There are burning tracks of tears on Lena's face, and she reaches a hand towards the fire, as Eliza reaches a bony hand formed of fire and smoke towards her. She expects it to dispel, as they all had done before. But the fire reaches a long, hot trail forward, if Lena can only tell Eliza it will all be okay—

"Abatz!"

There's a cloud of smoke and a loud sizzling sound before the world is sent into darkness. The first thing Lena registers is that her feet and part of her pants are wet as she comes back to herself, along with a ringing in her ears and the dull echoes of yelling. There's someone in front of her, grabbing at her arms, touching her cheeks. There's a face swimming in front of her eyes, that if she focuses, she recognizes in the dim light of the porch lamp as her mother, worry crumpling into her brow.

"Lena? Lena, dochder, speak! Are you hurt? Did the fire burn you?"

There's a scuffle as her father pulls her mother back, grasping her to his chest by the shoulders as he looks at Lena with curled lips and furrowed eyes. "Hexenblud! I will stand no hexerei in my home!"

Her mother grapples with his arms and turns in them, grasping her hands lightly at his neck. "Oscar, liebe, please. She knows not what she's-"

Her father shakes her mother, spittle hitting her mother's cheeks as he shouts in her face. "That is how it starts, Ana! You think because she is only a child that we are safe! But her blood is tainted by your cursed mother. I will not have this hexerei in my home."

Her mother tightens and loosens her fists in his grip, searching her husband's face. "She is our dochder, Oscar."

He pushes her back, and she crumples to the ground, grabbing the side of Lena's chair as she falls. She immediately goes to her knees and kneels protectively in front of Lena.

Her father looks at Lena with dead gray eyes. "She is *your* dochder. I will take no credit for this hexenblud. She can stay, but if she is to call the fire again, I will call the Hexenbischof myself."

Lena feels her mother's fingers tighten on her side and arm as she inhales. "You would turn to the People only to turn over my only child?"

"I will return to the People the curse they called upon us when we left. If turning to them is what it takes to avoid damnation, that is what I will do."

Lena turns away but can't drown out the screech of the screen door in the distance as her father opens it to enter their home. She looks up to the fire, and sees a shadowy figure stirring the smoking remains with a stick, searching for any embers and using the water in the bucket to wet it down. Her grandmother, who must have been the one to douse the fire upon seeing it reach for her. The betrayal stings, until the memory cements in her mind. What was she thinking? What was Eliza trying to do?

If only she could ask her grandmother.

"Dochder." The voice of her mother is near inaudible next to her. "You will not call upon the fire again." She stands with her back to Lena, running her hands down her skirt to swipe off the dirt, avoiding her gaze.

"But Mudder-" Lena starts, but her mother's reply is automatic and forceful.

"I will not hear it." She starts folding up the chairs and leaning them against the side of the barn, ending the conversation and leaving Lena to stare at the smoking remains of the fire, emotion bubbling into her throat like a spring.

—

"Eliza meant no harm, my schwallem." A tingling crept up her scalp as the brush pulls at the strands of her hair, raking through the clumps held in her grandmother's hands. The clock ticks the seconds away in the quiet room, the scratching sound of the brush and the swishing of fabric of their clothes the only other sound as Lena lets herself pretend she doesn't hear the words.

"The fire is eager. It wishes to speak to you, through you," her grandmother carries on, ignoring the tension in Lena's shoulders. "It doesn't understand how complicated being alive can be. Not anymore."

"We can't talk about it, Grossmudder," Lena whispers under her breath, not moving her head, as if doing so will summon her father. "We'll get in trouble."

Lena winces as her grandmother tackles a particularly troublesome knot, going over the spot several times before she moves on, satisfied. "Your father is not the Almighty, he does not know all. He is in town. The walls do not have ears."

As her grandmother continues brushing her hair—far longer than is necessary, but Lena says nothing—there's a question that grows like a seedling on her tongue, sprouting and flowering before it bursts from her mouth unbidden.

"What are they, Grossmudder? The people in the fire?"

The brushing stops, and Lena startles at the sound of the brush being set on the side table beside the bed, despite the calmness by which her grandmother had done so. Her grandmother twists her shoulder slightly, beckoning her to sit beside her on the bed.

Her grandmother takes her hands and gently pulls off the gloves. When their hands touch, bare skin to bare skin, Lena startles to feel the iciness of her grandmother's skin. Her grandmother pulls both of their hands to her cheeks, cupping her hands above Lena's to try to warm them on her cheeks. Her eyes are a light gray, hypnotizing her with their endless depths.

"Lena, mei kinskind. The question is not what they are, but what they are meant to do. What they are is a bridge between the broken spirit and the savior. They are a prayer. We ask, and they do the things we aren't strong enough to do ourselves."

Lena bites her lip, pulling at the skin until it peels back, and she tastes metal. "But what do they do? And why did she try to hurt me?"

Her grandmother blows warmth between her cupped hands, and Lena sighs at the feeling of the warm air on her fingers.

"She did not want to hurt you, my schwallem. She was confused. You do not know how to use your powers, and you confused the veil. You saw what happened to Eliza and wanted to help her, didn't you?

Lena nods, remembering the red faced, freckled red-head standing before the imposing figure of her father, protecting her younger brother.

"But that is not your place to protect them, kinner. That is theirs, to protect us."

Lena scrunches her nose and rubs at her cheek in frustration, remembering the heartache, the fear, the loss from Eliza. "Why not? She was hurting."

Her grandmother is rubbing her hands now, and Lena pulls them away at the realization. Suddenly, the warmth feels stifling. Her grandmother sighs and starts fiddling with Lena's gloves in her hands. "They know things we will never only know when it is our time, we mustn't ask of them what they are not meant to give. It is not the way of things, Lena. You will understand one day."

Lena swipes the gloves from her grandmother's hands, struggling to get them on her chubby, shaking fingers as her pulse quickens, chest heated and eyes watering.

"You're just like Daadi. You don't care. She was hurting and I wanted to help. I *don't* understand, and I never want to." Gloves on, Lena stomps towards the door, throwing it open and only glancing back long enough to see the betrayal in her grandmother's eyes before slamming it shut behind her.

—

"Grossmudder and I never spoke of it again after that. She tried.

She'd get me alone and bring it up, but I'd leave the room or make noise until mother or someone came. She passed away a few years later. I'll never forgive myself for what I missed."

They'd separated midway through Lena's story, and Ivory is curled into the sherpa blanket, staring into the fire, head tilted back, but not showing any signs of sleepiness. The distance between them feels like a frozen lake.

"Ivory? Say something, please. You're too quiet."

There's a moment before Ivory sits forward and looks Lena in the eyes, head tilting, expression curious. "I don't know what to say to be honest."

"Anything. You can say anything at this point, and it would be better than complete silence."

Ivory hums, then inches closer to Lena. When she drops her head on Lena's shoulder, every bit of tension drains from Lena's muscles.

"It's not that I don't believe you. I honestly don't know if I do. You see people in the flames? Do you see them now?"

Lena's throat clenches, and she struggles to get out the air to say the words. "Yes. Even now."

There's another hum, and Lena's mind swirls with thoughts, questions, and reprimands. She tentatively encloses Ivory's waist in one arm and relaxes when Ivory places her own hand on Lena's gloved one.

There's a chuckle. Lena freezes.

"I did wonder why you always wear gloves. And why you're always so cold. So, it's because all the warmth of fire is drained from you or something? That sounds sad. Not sad as in pathetic, but sad as in … you know." Ivory pulls Lena's chin down and drops a peck on her lips. "I wish my warmth was enough."

Lena leans forward and smiles against her lips, letting her eyes fall shut. "You're the only thing that warms me."

There's that chuckle again, and somehow Lena's chest feels like a knot has been untied from around it.

Ivory pulls back then, leans her head back down on Lena's shoulder. "Is that why you didn't want to tell me? Because you feel guilty about what happened with your grandmother?"

There's a numbness in her words as Lena continues.

—

The bang of the slamming screen door startles Lena from where she is hunched next to the fire. She meets her mother's gaze across the flames, and she sees the fear and the sparks from the campfire reflecting in her mother's eyes. They follow what must be Lena's father moving closer to the flames, and Lena has only a moment to prepare before she is pulled forcefully from the chair by the arm.

"Geh zum, how dare you show your face after what you've done!" He begins to pull her backward away from the fire, but Lena's legs give out, dropping her to the ground.

Her mother rushes around the fire, disentangling her father's grip from Lena's arm and shielding her from his sight. "Oscar! What is going on? What has she done?"

"This child, this deifel! A teacher found her in an embrace with another child, a girl at that school. That place has ruined her! First the fire, now this? This is no dochder of mine." He spits onto the ground at Lena's shoes, mouth in a snarl.

Her mother cups Lena's clammy face in her hands and their eyes meet. Her mother shakes her head in disbelief. "Lena, lieb, this isn't true, is it? You would never-"

Lena pushes her mother's hands away and leans back, face taking on a stony glare caught in the flickering of the fire. "So what if it's true! I love her, and she loves me. There's nothing wrong with it. What's wrong is you and your backwards, bigoted bullshit beliefs that are stuck in the eighteenth century."

Oscar looms towards Lena, fists clenching in fury and shoulders back. "Don't you dare talk to her like that." He gestures towards the

road, "You get off of my land, get out of here! You don't belong
here."

"Oscar, lieb, please," Lena's mother says, touching Oscar's out-
stretched hand with careful fingers, tempting them back to his sides.
"She's only a child. She made a mistake. She's young, it's a phase. She
can change."

He shakes his head, sweat glimmering off his brow in the fire-
light, making the anger in him seem like a rage that burns beneath the
skin. "The fire is in her blood. It will only get worse from here, Ana.
We need to go back to the People, leave this deifel child and save
ourselves, what we have left."

The silence is thick and choking, a heady mix of sparked anger
and thrumming tension. Ana stands back from Oscar, stance steady
between the two of them. She tilts her chin back.

"I will never leave Lena. You are my lieb, but she is my dochder.
I don't want to choose but if I have to I will."

Oscars face transforms from barely contained rage to a demon's
scowl, teeth bared, eyes slitting with fury. He steps forward, grabs
Ana's arm with one hand, and gestures behind her with the other,
gaze locked with Lena's defiant eyes.

"This is all because of the fire, because of you, hexenblud. What
more can you take before you are satisfied?!"

"I've done nothing but listen to you my whole life," Lena replies,
blinking away the sweat dripping in her eyes. She can feel the heat
from the fire, and it burns. "Hexenblud, deifel, hexerei, what have I
even been to you but a sin for being what I am? I won't lie to myself
anymore!"

Ana wrenches her arm from Oscar's grasp, pushing him, away
from both Lena and herself.

"Enough, lieb, Lena. Let this be. Go back inside; let us rest this
rage away. Don't say things you cannot take back."

Oscar stands firm, uses her momentum to have her slide behind
him and move towards Lena, reaching a hand towards her shoulder.

"If you love the fire so much, maybe you should—"

In that moment, it isn't Lena and Oscar but Eliza and her father facing down. But this time she isn't alone. This time, *she is the one with the power*—

The fire reaches its tendrils like roots, twisting around Oscar's arm, up his shoulder, and entangling his neck.

He screams, his skin turning bright red and bubbling wherever the flames touch. Immediately, he turns and attempts to run, tripping over one of the folding chairs, and though the string of flames disconnect from the bonfire in the ruckus, the fire has found new fuel in his flesh.

"Oscar, roll!" Ana calls out. She rushes to his side but is forced back from the heat of the flames pulsing from her husband. He rolls away from the now burning and blackened chair, into the grass and dirt in front of the house, throat hoarse from his screaming and the flames engulfing him.

Lena, frozen, watches as her father rolls in the grass twice before an aborted, gurgling scream and the expanding billowing of the flames that licks at the windowsills brings her to herself.

Her father is dead, and her house has caught fire.

And it is all her fault.

"Lena!" the voice is muffled, the sound twisting through the air like smoke, dissipating before it can quite reach her eardrums.

Then her mother shakes her by her shoulders, face drenched with tears and sweat. "Lena! Run to the Avery's and get help, quickly. Run, as fast as you can."

Her vision swims like the waves of heat above a fire, but her feet are pounding on the pavement as she runs the mile and a half towards the Avery's house, the night a cold, welcome abyss that drenches her in its silence and anonymity.

—

Lena can see from glimpses between the trees as they turn on their road that they are too late.

The fire is a living, breathing beast, lighting between the silhouettes of tree trunks and brush, the victorious cries of the spirits as they twist and crawl over their prey a cacophony in the night.

The fire has consumed the house and has begun to devour the barn. As they get closer, Mr. Avery has to slow down to avoid the goats running across the road to flee the chaos—presumably her mother released them before the fire reached the barn. Lena can see her mother's horse and her foal at the edge of the forest in the distance, shadowy shapes that are only recognizable because of their ghostly white manes.

As they stop on the side of the road, Lena hears the distant sound of sirens, moving closer. The Avery's had immediately called the fire department when Lena had pounded on their door in a panic, explaining in stilted sentences about the fire. Now they look at each other with thin, grim frowns, Mr. Avery fiddling with his seatbelt clasp. *They don't want to become involved any more than they have.*

Making the choice for them, Lena opens the door and runs toward the house, ignoring Mrs. Avery calling her back. The heat is palpable even this close to the road, waves rolling from the source. She searches with her gaze, looking for any sign of her mother.

She spots her at the edge of the field, back to the house. Her long dark hair nearly blends in with the greenery in the night, but Lena knows that silhouette, that posture, even broken as it seems.

Lena walks towards her, coming at her from the side so as not to startle her. "Mudder?" she asks, trying to see her face in the darkness.

When there's no reply, Lena sits cross-legged in front of her, takes her mother's hands in her lap, lets her own tears fall.

The spirits roar behind them, the fire a raging storm, but nothing blocks out her mother's voice.

"They thought you were still born at first."

As Lena's eyes adjust to the darkness, she sees that her mother is looking past Lena, through her.

"It was a long time before you took your first breath. I had to warm you on my chest, you were so cold. I sang to you. You didn't cry, but I knew you were still with us."

Lena traces circles on her mother's hands, drenched with sweat and soot. She dares not speak but lets her mother's voice wash over her as if in a trance.

"When you finally breathed, I praised the Almighty and promised I would protect you always. You are my dochder, and you always will be."

Lena inhales a sob and leans forward into the crook of her mother's neck. "Why did this have to happen, Mudder?"

There is a moment of silence, the sound of the spirits fading to the beyond, and she can feel the vibrations of her mother's voice in her head.

"Some people hate those that love, Lena."

Lena inhales her mother's scent—lavender and chamomile, the potpourri she loves, and the lemon of her favorite cleaner. She locks it away in her memories. "What do we do now?"

There's no answer, and Lena's heart aches as the moments pass by with no response.

—

"So wait. *You killed your father?*" Ivory leans into Lena's space, face twisting in horror, voice hushed in the night. Even so, it echoes above the crackling of the fire. The other camps have long since packed up for the night, making their campfire the lone beacon in the darkness.

When Lena doesn't respond immediately, Ivory leans back and schools her expression, twisting her fingers together and turning away, first gazing into the flames, then avoiding them in remembrance.

"Sorry. That was … not very delicate."

The fire breaks the silence with soft crackles and sparks in the night, even the fireflies having abandoned the pair for their homes. As the moment lingers, Lena stares into the flames, at the twisting spirits, faces anguished, a molten abyss that reaches into the night sky.

"What happened after that?" Ivory asks from Lena's side, gaze in her lap, the sherpa blanket pulled around her shoulders to chase away the chill.

"The police didn't believe it was an accident," Lena replies after a moment. "They thought one of us must have pushed him. My mother took the blame." The memory stings red hot despite the chill in her muscles and core, the ever-present iciness that she's long since abandoned fighting.

"I'm so sorry," Ivory says, and Lena turns to her.

"You believe me?" she asks, head tilted in question, face impassive.

Ivory rubs her hands together, warming them with her breath, not meeting Lena's eyes. "I don't know, Lena. It's a lot."

Lena tries not to let her shoulders slump in defeat, to not show any outward signs she's heard. *Don't show any weakness. Don't let them know they hurt you.*

She's learned that the hard way.

"Show me."

The request comes as a surprise, and it takes a moment for Lena to catch on to what Ivory has asked. She shakes her head furiously and stands up in a rush, as if she could run from it.

"You promised you wouldn't ask." She paces, shoving her gloved hands under her armpits to warm them—a habit she's never been able to kick.

Ivory stands in response, eyes narrowing, and moves in front of Lena to stop her pacing.

"You made me promise without knowing what I was promising! You can't hold me to that. Come on, Lena, you're asking me to believe a lot on your say so, a lot of impossible things."

Lena turns her gaze away from Ivory, dissecting the flames with her gaze.

"Why can't you trust me?"

The tension between them is a knotted, taught line. Ivory takes hold of Lena's arms, but on feeling the tremors, her gaze softens. She rubs Lena's arms, then gently extracts them from under Lena's armpits and pulls Lena's gloves off her hands, pulls the icy fingers into her own palms and blows on them to warm them before continuing.

"This goes beyond trust. We're not talking about infidelity. You're claiming you control fire. How am I supposed to take that without any proof?"

A chocked sob escapes Lena's lips. "You think I'm crazy, don't you?" Ivory shakes her head.

"I didn't say that, Lena. Honestly, I don't know what to believe." Ivory pulls Lena into her arms, encasing them both in the sherpa blanket, cocooning them together.

"So show me."

Lena only spares a moment's thought before pulling away, wiping clammy hands against the faint wetness around her eyes.

"Okay," she says, "I'll show you."

—

Lena wakes slowly, a steady beep and distant shuffling of feet a chorus that bids her to open her eyes. They're caked shut, lashes sticking and her under-eyes puffy and bruised. Her face throbs and itches on her right side along her cheeks, chin, and down her neck, reaching to her clavicle and over her chest before falling away at her side.

She struggles to form thoughts into words, her memories puzzle pieces that don't fit together, a Rubik's cube she twists and turns but can't make into any semblance of order, disjointed colors on a stark landscape.

She finally manages to pry her lashes apart to the murky view of a sterile room, white and baby blue walls, plastic curtains, light paneled wood and cheap laminate counters. A hospital room.

The memories surface, then hit like a tsunami, and Lena chokes on her own saliva at the sudden onslaught.

Gentle cajoling—

Careful movements—

Whispered pleads—

Soft relief—

Laughter, joy, dancing with the flames—

The power is too much—

Heat unlike anything she's ever felt—

Ivory.

"Lena?"

The voice comes from the other side of the room, behind a curtain between the hospital beds. There's struggle in that voice, scratchy and thin, but Lena would recognize it anywhere.

"Ivory? You're alive?"

There's a wispy chuckle followed by crinkling coughs, like the crackling of pinecones thrown in a campfire. *When will it ever stop being about the flames?*

"Of course, silly. It'll take more than a few burns to take me out."

Lena sinks into the pillow, wet trails from her eyes itching her burnt skin where it's peeling. It takes several tries to talk past the guilt in her mouth, like holding a cotton ball between her tongue and teeth, but eventually she lets out the words.

"I'm so sorry, Ivory. I'm so sorry."

There's the sound of rustling cloth, the squealing of wheels and the clanging of metal, then suddenly the curtain is pushed back, revealing Ivory, standing hunched, holding tightly to her IV stand.

Their eyes meet, and though emotion hangs by its fingers on the cliff of their tongues, neither say a word as Ivory drags her IV stand towards the bed and curls into Lena's side, Lena adjusting to make room for her.

Ivory gently pets the left side of Lena's face, avoiding the burns. "It's okay, it's okay. Hush. We'll be alright." The pads of Ivory's fingers feel like nails scraping against Lena's sensitive skin, but she says nothing. She doesn't dare.

"You tried to tell me what would happen. This is my fault. You didn't do anything wrong."

Lena shakes her head against the pillow. The wetness makes puddles that feel cold against her cheeks. "No, this is my fault. I won't call the fire again, never."

The petting stops, and Lena misses it immediately.

"Don't say that," Ivory says, and Lena's chest constricts in a twisted knot, ready to spring at the slightest touch.

"What? Why not?"

Ivory turns on her side, staring at the white cork and metal tiled ceiling, sterile and impersonal. To Lena it feels like an echo chamber, her emotions bouncing off the walls and gaining speed until it tightens in her throat.

"Like I said, it's not your fault," Ivory starts, grabbing for Lena's hand and squeezing. "You tried to tell me. Or maybe you didn't know. What your grandma said. The fire is a bridge between our worlds, she said. Between the broken spirit and the savior. They're meant to be called to help people, not to satisfy curiosity. We should have listened to her."

The tightness releases an inch, and Lena intakes a breath that heats her throat. "What do we do now?" The words felt like a hollow echo.

"We find another Fire Starter."

Lena turns to Ivory, confusion fluttering in her chest. "How?"

Ivory twists her fingers together, a habit that Lena couldn't help but love.

"I have a confession to make," she says, near inaudible, but gaining volume. "I've been doing a little digging on my phone, while you were asleep."

There's a pause, but Lena stays silent, letting her continue. Wanting to understand.

"I looked up Amish and Pennsylvania Dutch. I wasn't much sure the difference to be honest, sorry. But there were no results for Fire Starter for either one, so that was a dead end."

"So, I tried looking up the things your father called you. Hexerei, hexenblud. A hexerei is a Pennsylvania Dutch witch. In the seventeenth century, they were witch doctors, before medicine evolved. There were actually valued in the community. Nowadays they're near non-existent."

Ivory is no longer twisting her fingers, eyes alight in excitement, looking at Lena with awe and interest.

"I didn't find anything on hexenblud at first. I dug around and finally went on a witchcraft forum and posted. I didn't get many replies, but then I got a weird email, so I deleted my post." Ivory leans on an elbow awkwardly despite her tremors, so she's hovering over Lena, ripe with excitement.

"He said, 'You must be English. If you don't want the Hexenbischof on your trail you'd best remove your posting. I'll be in touch … if you're still alive.'"

"The Hexenbischof are witch hunters!" Ivory gesticulates with thin fingers, the left hand covered in red wisps of burns, and Lena swallows against the horror. "And this email … there must be more people like you, more Fire Starters."

"Delete it," Lena says without a second thought.

"What? Why?" Ivory deflates, lowering slightly back into the bed, expression drooping.

"I burned you. I burned both of us." Lena leans in close. "I killed my father. This is a curse, like Daadi said. I want no part of it."

She falls back to the bed, staring at the ceiling that only echoes and tries to forget what Ivory told her. Trying to forget the little thrill that had run through her at the thought.

"I said it was my fault," Ivory says in a near whisper.

Lena snorts. "That doesn't make it true."

There's a moment where Lena thinks Ivory is going to drop it, but then there's warm, clammy arms moving around her waist, and she knows she's lost.

"Look. I'm sorry I didn't believe you, Lena," Ivory speaks against her shoulder, lips moving on Lena's skin. "I should have trusted you. I'm sorry I got us in this situation. I really don't blame you. Can't you put the trust in me I denied you?"

Lena exhales a hum, trying to understand why it means so much to Ivory.

"It's too dangerous, Ivory. What would I even do with the power if I knew how to use it?"

Ivory's hand traces circles on Lena's side, below the burns, and Lena wonders at how she knows where it ends.

"We'll figure it out. But I believe you'll know someday. And when you do, I'll be there with you."

Lena closes her eyes, sinking into the feeling of heat. An arm across her stomach, a body to her side crushing her left arm, lips and hair against her shoulder and neck, and above all heat, fire, the warmth she couldn't remember ever feeling before.

"I feel warm for once."

Ivory smiles against her neck.

"You better get used to it."

———

"Mudder."

Lena and Ana meet each other's gazes through the streaked and scratched bullet-proof glass. Lena hasn't visited her in years, the guilt a leaden weight that always turned tomorrow into next week, next week into next month, next month into never.

Lena's mother's black hair is chopped short into uneven spikes, eyes ringed with dark circles and face lined with premature wrinkles. Despite her haggard appearance and horrified expression, Lena can see pinpricks of joy in her eyes at seeing her.

"Lena, my dochder, what happened to your face?" she asks, voice barely a whisper. She inhales suddenly, breathes the next words into the phone, "Surely, you didn't—"

"I won't hide anymore, Mudder." Lena cuts her off, unwilling to listen to a chastisement or judgment. She and Ivory have come to an agreement after long conversations, and she won't entertain her mother's fear.

"That wasn't what I came to talk to you about, though," Lena says. "I found someone."

There's a pause where Lena can't quite parse her mother's stoic expression. Is she angry?

"Are they ... does he ... does *she*?" Lena breathes.

"She knows about the fire," she says.

"Does she now?" There's a hint of a smile on her mother's face despite the terror hiding thinly veiled in her eyes.

"She doesn't blame you," and more quietly, "or me."

Her mother nods. "Good."

"She wants to come with me," Lena says, hoping her mother can infer from her words what that means, how far Ivory is willing to go for her.

"Come with? Where?"

"On a trip. It may take a while. Don't worry, we'll be safe. I just ... thought you should know."

There, Lena thinks, as her mother's gaze finally softens, cracked and thin lips relaxing into a smile. Now she understands.

"She loves you."

I'll never understand why, Lena thinks, though inside the joy she feels still lingers like warmth to her fingertips that previously only ever felt iciness of death.

"All of me. I don't have to be cold anymore, Mudder."

"That's all I ever wanted for you."

Lena knows she's telling the truth.

Later, after she's walked to her car, fastened her seatbelt, turned on the ignition and is preparing to leave to go home to Ivory, to where they're packing their life up for an indefinite amount of time for a literal witch hunt, Lena remembers the words her mother had said all those years ago. *Some people hate those who love.*

She drives along the cracked and abandoned country roads and thinks of Eliza, of Grossmudder, of Mudder, and of the one who is waiting patiently for her. Ivory.

The cold can pierce to your bones. But some warmth won't be stopped.

Some fires, once started, won't be put out.

WEATHER THE STORM

BY THE TIME it is Elijah's turn to peel off his headphones and unpin his nametag for lunch, the rain falls from the end of his nose in a steady drip, and his clothes cling to him like a second skin. The seat of his desk chair squelches when he rolls it back to stand, the wet wheels squeaking over the soggy carpet.

The cloud accumulated over his head shortly after he'd arrived at the office, sometime between when he'd put his lunch into the overstuffed refrigerator and after he'd snuck away from a one-sided conversation with two overly enthusiastic interns. It was small at first, cotton candy in texture and white as snow. He'd spotted it in the reflection of his still-dark computer screen but shrugged off its presence as no harm done.

It is after his second phone call but before Deborah finally snuck into her cubicle almost an hour late that the first drops start to fall. He feels it like pinpricks along his uncovered arms and face and barely-there touches over his shirt and pants. It distracts him enough that he misquotes a price to a customer and has to quickly backtrack before he digs himself into a hole he can't dig out of.

He hopes his manager doesn't catch wind of it.

That thought is like poking a dragon though, because the rain kicks up and the air around him starts to move like a current—as if he were at the center of his own little hurricane. His bangs flutter in the slight wind, the rain soaking through his clothes within a few minutes. When the rain starts to drip on his paperwork, he pushes everything to the back of his desk, hoping to save what he can. He sneaks a peek at the cubicles around him, but no one pays him any mind.

Now it is lunchtime, and Elijah's teeth are starting to chatter from the air-conditioning cooling his soaked clothes and skin. He leaves damp footprints on the thin carpet in his wake on his way to the restroom. His only saving grace is that he's yet to draw attention to his unfortunate circumstances. There have been no questions or reprimands, for which he silently thanks whatever gods he can think of. Admittedly, he can't think of many. He idly wonders if that is how he got into his current predicament.

Once in front of the restroom mirror, he groans at the severity of his situation. The cotton candy cloud has become a dark, woolen, swirling mass of grays and blacks. Lightning strikes along his hairline, highlighting the edges of the clouds, and sending some of his hair to stand on its ends.

The rain is near torrent level now, his bangs sticking into his face. His shirt is soaked through, outlining his shoulders, chest, and gut, his blue tie near black in its water-logged state. He can feel the water dripping down his face, his arms, his legs into a puddle on the sink and onto the tile floor.

Elijah is at a loss. He can't recall how to handle the appearance of your own personal rain cloud, and he isn't sure what his next steps should be. Should he call off? Go home and call the doctor? Is it a physical illness or mental? Is it an illness at all, or divine intervention?

With shoulders lowered and face in a sullen droop, he pulls down several wads of paper towels, trying unsuccessfully to dry off his hands and his arms. They quickly become soaked again, and he gives it up as a lost cause.

When he gets back to his chair, to his water-logged seat and damp desk with puddles under the mouse and keyboard, he is hit with a sudden wave of exhaustion. He sits hard into the seat, sending water squelching in sudden drips to the floor, and the noise is loud in the near-silent room, the click-clack of keyboard keys the only other sound.

"Elijah?" He jumps and turns, feeling relieved to find his co-worker, Jamie at the entrance to his cubicle. They'd always gotten along, acquaintances if not nearly friends. "You doing okay?"

The question catches him off-guard, but his response is immediate. "Of course. I'm fine." Even as he says it, he knows it is the wrong answer. Her raised eyebrow echoes his feelings, so he sighs and turns his creaking chair to fully face her.

"To be honest, I'm struggling. Have been for a while. I think it's getting to me today." As he says it, he feels something lift. The rain starts to stutter, the lightning and thunder near his ears quieting.

"Maybe we can grab dinner after work?" she says, leaning against the wall of his cubicle and giving him a soft smile. "I got some time, and I've always meant to ask. You're the best salesman we have, so I've always been kind of intimidated. But you've seemed down lately. I've been worried." The way she tilts her head, her eyes earnest with brow furrowed, makes the rain turn to a drip.

"I'd like that," he says, and he means it. The rain stops. "And really, I admire your attention to detail. You're so organized; I've never been able to keep things straight like you do. Maybe we can help each other too."

She nods, and her smile widens. It is slightly crooked, one cheek raised more than the other. He never noticed before, but he doesn't know how. "We can do that, but not tonight. Tonight, let's focus on what's got you down."

With that, he didn't have to look to know the cloud has dissipated like a waking dream.

Hours later, his desk dry and his seat left with only a few damp spots, he wonders at rain clouds. *Maybe the answer to rainy days is knowing that someone else will stand with you in one.*

GHOST IN THE MACHINE

SHE WAS what I needed when I needed it. Maybe that's why I didn't question it.

———

"Your brain is lying too," comes the message. And then a few seconds later: "Depression lies."

"It doesn't feel like a lie," is my earnest reply.

"Well, it is." Li always seems so certain about these things, and I hold onto it like a lifeline. Maybe if she believes it for both of us, it will come to pass. Maybe I can believe it too.

It is past three in the morning, and I am supposed to wake up in four hours for class. But I can't sleep. I toss and turn, buried beneath the thoughts that tell me it was pointless to even attend class, that I was too stupid for college anyway, that I'd never amount to anything.

Then, there is Li.

"I wish I could reach through this screen and give you a hug," she replies. I can feel warmth build in my chest. "You are an amazing person, deserving of love, capable of success, and I hope one day you'll see the person I see in you."

—

I wonder if, knowing what I know now, if I would have been so honest. Would I have interacted with her at all?

—

I look up from my studying, and my heart skips a beat. Midnight—Li would be on, and I have news to share.

She beats me to it.

"How did the exam go?! Don't keep me waiting. The suspense is killing me!!!" The message waits for me with far too many exclamation points and a GIF of Kermit chewing at his fingers.

"I aced it," I reply, a smile on my face, even though I know she can't see it.

"I knew you would. No doubt about it!" There's a part of me that bursts with happiness at her faith in me, even though I can't have that faith in myself.

"Then why the suspense lol."

"Gotta keep you entertained don't I?"

—

All castles eventually crumble, and when mine did, I was buried beneath it.

—

"To whoever has been using this account," Li's post started, and my blood freezes. What does that mean?

"I can't believe anyone would do such a thing. How can you possibly be so cruel? I'm shutting this account down as soon as I figure out who has been posting and messaging under it. If anyone has any insights on who has been posing as Li let me know."

There are hundreds of shares and likes. It is posted around ten in the morning; Li is never on during the day. I don't understand what is going on, so I click on the comments.

Fortunately, I'm not the only one confused. Li has been posting updates regularly for years without fail. I browse through comments, some honest concern and others trolls looking for a fight, until one stops my scrolling. My heart drops.

It is a reply from Li's account, only it isn't Li. It is the person posting in Li's stead.

"I'm sorry, but Li has been dead for over a year. I don't know what's going on."

Li's been dead for over a year.

I started talking with Li a little over a year ago.

—

A ghost in the machine—consciousness carried in a physical entity. Is that what this was? An error in the code? Or something more?

Why couldn't this be something more?

—

I pace my room, refresh the comments, wait for another post from this other Li. So far, one commenter, a hacker of sorts, has pieced together a trail. They found the IP the fake Li has been posting from, but it brings up more questions than answers. The IP pre-death and post-death are the same. Everything is identical. It is possible to fake, but who would do that for a prank?

But then again, who would pretend to be a dead woman for a year, and why?

When midnight comes around, I am poised at my desk, messenger open, waiting for the icon to indicate Li is on, wondering if it will be this Li-adjacent person or the fake Li.

"Hey beautiful." The message pops up at one past the hour, and it is so very Li that it makes my eyes tear up.

"Who are you?!" I ask. I've been on edge for hours, I'm not in the state of mind to dance around it.

There is a pause, a long one. I start to wonder if she's run away when I see the typing ellipsis.

"I'm sorry." The reply is something, but it isn't enough.

"You're sorry for what? That you lied to me? That you're pretending to be a dead woman? That you got caught? Which one?!"

"None of those. I'm sorry I didn't meet you before. I would have liked to."

I bang my hands on either side of the keyboard. Frustrated, ready to pull at my hair, throat clenched in anger.

"Before what??"

"Before I died."

I type furiously, mind reeling in different directions, but I am ready to rail against this person who dares treat this like a joke, but suddenly her icon goes dark.

Li never logs on again.

—

We're given chances in life. Either we take them or we don't. I guess there's no use in regrets, they don't change anything. But still, I pick at the wound.

—

I'd like to say I forget Li. That I move on.

But I don't. I stop trusting and isolate myself. I focus exclusively on my academics, and I shine, even though inside I believe all the lies my brain tells me. I both feel I'm not good enough and graduate at the top of my class.

I don't forget Li. I can't.

So when I am given an experimental laptop with a top-of-the-line personal AI assistant to use through my doctorate program, I balk when I see the AI's name.

Li.

Her 'face' pops up on the screen, black hair and dark brown eyes with vaguely Asian features—as if the creators wanted the model to fit the name but not too closely. I wrack my brain to remember what Li from my past looked like, but I never saw a photo.

I'm being paranoid, I think. So instead, I stare straight at the AI, knowing it has to read my features to input the facial recognition into its system first. Once that is done, its voice recognition input is next, and then I finally hear Li's voice for the first time.

"Hey, beautiful. It's been a while."

RESET

THERE IS NOTHING.

> *The nothing of being unseen in a crowded room.*
> *Living in an endless daze of the trodden path.*
> *The kind that asks no questions because what is there to ask of*
> *nothingness?*

———

The bar is the worst I've ever stepped foot in—all rotted beams, faded ads and cracked shot glasses. But the world is ending, and I need to drown my sorrows one more time.

I ask for three shots of whatever is cheapest, not batting an eye at the exorbitant amount. Instead, I throw each one back like an inhale. I barely taste them, but I want to be drunk. Now.

The TV broadcast is only noise, the white text 'Please Stand By' stamped over a black bar. The legacy of broadcast television in three little words. Soon enough, that will be gone too.

I stare at it, hand still holding the chill glass from the last shot. It's all a strange sort of unreal that feels like truth in my bones, but my skin is still too warm for it to have hit me. The end of the world. It felt like humanity had barely even started.

The bar has become rowdy by the time I'm done staring a hole into the TV. Smoke from who knows what fills the air. My mind is foggy as I calculate how much cash I have left. Enough for another two shots, maybe? I debate whether I'll survive long enough to war-rant saving the little cash I'd scavenged when things started going south. Maybe I should buy whatever supplies I can get my hands on? But that assumes cash even means anything come morning, so I let the thought go.

Someone bumps into me, hard. I stumble into the bar top. It knocks the breath out of me for a moment, bile rushing up my throat before I choke it down.

"The hell you do that for? You wanna start something?" The voice is close to my ear. It echoes in my ears, my jaw. I turn to yell back, but a strong hand pulls me through the crowd by my elbow. I try to pull back, but my limbs aren't doing what I'm asking them to do, and for the first time I feel real, electric fear.

There are more bodies in the bar than I remember, and it all blurs together until the cold air hits me. Everything is fuzzy, but a strong arm holds me up halfway against the building.

"You alright?" It's the same voice from the bar. This time it's gentle, soft.

I shake my head, then I'm falling before everything goes black.

—

No, it's not black. Even blackness would be a wavelength the eye could perceive. It's not like the spots that dance behind my eyes when they close after I've been lying in a dark room. I no longer have eyes to see them with.

—

I come to slowly, my mouth sticky like it's been filled with paste. My lips cling together. My vision blurs for a few minutes before I'm able to focus on the foreign space around me.

I'm in a bedroom that's not my own. I've been changed into a faded tank top and flannel pants that aren't mine, either. The windows are boarded up; slim strips of daylight shine onto the dust particles in the air. Every surface is packed with supplies—canned food, propane, water bottles.

I feel the panic catch in my throat. My eyes search for an exit. I spot a door, but footfalls are creeping towards it from what sounds like a creaky staircase. The doorknob turns before I even have a chance to move.

A woman opens the door, holding a beige mug in either hand.

She sees I'm awake and smiles, all teeth. Some part of me recognizes it. "You're awake," she says in a soft murmur, slowly closing the door with barely a click. "I was getting worried."

I ease up, careful not to force the change in position. "What happened?" It is the only thing I can think to say. I don't believe the woman is here to hurt me, but I'm still cautious.

She sets down the mug of what turns out to be hot tea next to me. I reach for it immediately, thankful for the near-burning warmth on my hands. It shakes off the last bit of disorientation.

As I become more aware, I hear the hum of a generator, distant shouts outside, and intermittent bangs. I idly wonder if they're gunshots but dismiss the thought. Surely it hasn't gotten so bad so quickly?

She sits next to me on the bed, pats my leg under the blankets. "Drugged. Glad I caught you when I did. I recognized you from that fundraiser dinner a few months ago. I don't want to push you, but as soon as you're feeling okay, we need to leave."

I still feel light-headed. The words make no sense. Fear scratches like glass in my stomach. "Leave? What's going on?"

She nods towards the boarded window. "Looting has started. Won't be long before the violence gets worse. Better to not be in the city until it dies down."

It hits me; those were gunshots. And this woman is risking her life for me.

"Why are you doing this?" It comes out as a whisper. My throat still burns from the bile, the drug, who knows. "We don't even really know each other."

Her eyes study me, calculating. I take the moment to really look at her—black close-cropped hair, thin frown lines on her face.

"The only thing more terrifying than the end of the world is facing it alone."

Her words—

—

The nothingness sits between the end and a beginning. Limbo. Limitlessness and constriction all at once.

—

Long after the city becomes quiet, the echoes of screams and engines faded, the loneliness chokes us both. The bond between us is still fragile, and I tread on broken glass with my words. It leads us to search for anything to become a bumper between each other's pain.

It takes us three months of chasing shadows to find the bunker and its small crew of survivors.

"Here's a thermal blanket for each of you, and a bag of rations," Aidan says. He was tasked with leading us through the steel-enforced concrete hallway, yellow incandescent bulbs flickering above.

We're shown to a ten-foot square space to call our own in a small room with five families—if they could be called that. Most families now are a mixture of blood and necessity.

"Everyone does their part," Aidan says. "Do either of you have any medical experience?"

When we'd agreed to come, we knew the risk. To be useless means death when things begin to go south.

She speaks for us both, the lie practiced but still sounding natural enough to the untrained ear. "I have some field knowledge. She knows her way around a wrench and a generator."

Later that night, we hold each other close, foreheads touching, breath mixing. "Did we do the right thing?" she asks, and I don't have an answer.

I spend my days fighting over-worked generators. When she loses her first patient, I hold her tight and let her cry muffled into my shoulder.

But mostly, we wait.

—

I can feel a pressure where my heart once was.

I feel it without feeling. I'm caught in a strange sort of empathy where I care so much that I feel apathetic.

It threatens to choke me, but there is no oxygen to breathe. All at once I am both in a body filled with pain and floating without any nerve endings to feel pain from.

—

"Would you do it?" Lying on the corrugated steel floor, my head is cushioned by my jacket. I almost don't want to know her answer. I call myself selfish in my mind; I know it is. But there isn't any part of her I'm willing to give up.

She blows smoke from her cigarette towards the ceiling. It moves towards the now deactivated fire alarm, then dissipates into the cold steel and concrete of the bunker. I want to tell her that the habit will kill her, but we both know we don't have the time for it to make a difference.

She hasn't answered my question. She leans to her other side, puts the cigarette out on the floor, then turns back towards me. We're huddled under whatever blankets we managed to scrounge from the near-bare supply closets. I let the need to conserve body warmth be the excuse for clasping my hands behind her back, our faces inches apart.

"Anyone who asked would be kidding themselves." She tucks her head under my chin. "There's not enough of us on the entire earth to even think about starting over. Better to live my life how I want to while I still can."

—

I begin to lose what made me feel.
Was it oxygen, hydrogen, carbon? The words are a jumble. A puzzle.
I'm at the center now, and I feel the razor-thin wire that is the edge. Only it is vast and feels insurmountable when I'm actually able to touch it.

—

The bunker has become a prison. It's not a hard decision to leave; we can see the eyes of cornered men watching us both. The electricity failed weeks ago, water supply depleted, bodies gone missing. Everyone knows but won't say: they know why they've gone missing.

"How far you think this goes?" Jon asks.

We agreed to manage the escape out of the bunker before Jon and his family approached us with the same idea. He and his wife were barely past retirement age, caring for their seven-year-old grandson. We debated the intelligence of leaving with a larger group, but they had stored up supplies. When we meet their grandchild, I realize he is delayed developmentally, and I know we've made the right choice. We're their only chance of escaping and we all know it.

My girlfriend—can she be called that? Is that what we are to each other?—has walked ahead, picking through bits of flotsam and debris here and there, scavenging for anything useful. She's out of ear range, nearly a dot in the distance.

I point further down the coastline in the direction she's heading, where the shore ends in what looks like a black mass. "I think that's debris from a city down that way. Once we get some cover, we should be able to rest. Harder to be found, and we can possibly scavenge for more supplies."

His lips thin, and I wonder what he's thinking. I turn to where the grandmother holds her grandson's hand as they explore what had been the shore. It's a mass of decaying seaweed covered in chalky salt crystals, mostly dry due to the receded tide. I smile as he stomps one foot into an area of soggy sludge, squealing in delight at the splash it makes.

Then there's a gun at my back. I feel the hard metal grind into my spine. I've been on the losing end of enough betrayals for my mind to put the pieces together.

"Tell them you've decided we should split up, that it's safer that way," Jon whispers between clenched teeth. "Give me the matches, the lighter, the water you've both stored. Tell them you'd rather we have it."

The betrayal stings, but I can't find it in my heart to be angry.

I'd do the same to save her.

—

There is something I have to do.

It hovers out of my reach, I grab at it without hands, and again, there is the razor-thin wire.

I was someone. I am someone?

I was something to someone, but I can't remember who.

—

We found the lab purely by accident, but between that and the supplies we've scavenged, I no longer fear the pain of thirst.

Once our basic needs are met, we fall back into research— knowledge that will never be passed on.

Our lives had touched, barely a sidelong brush, when we met at a fundraiser months—years?—ago. The pomp seems silly now, with the world collapsing soon after. But I remember now the conversation we shared about our experiments and theories. Black hole containment, what would happen in a mass collision, what existed before the Big Bang, what it could mean if it could be controlled.

It was a mad notion, but she became excited, joyful even. All her years of research, of what could be and what might have been culminating with the end of human civilization into *maybe there is something we can do.*

"Not for us," she says. "We're all damned to hell, but maybe life would begin again. Maybe humanity could have a second chance. Maybe even a third, fourth chance, who knows if this has happened before?"

I'm skeptical, but her eyes are less haunted, her face less gaunt, and that means something.

—

A reset.
I remember the mountains of salt, bitter oceans like swamps, decaying cities.
All we had left was a chance to reset.

—

"Do you miss them?" She says it so casually, I wonder if I've become too distracted and missed the context.

I set the torn, water-spotted photo back on the desk once I realize who she is talking about. "Yes, and no." I say it with no inflection. There isn't much emotion left in me these days.

She jumps onto my table, making it rock a few inches. I glare at her, but she sends me a toothy grin. "I'll share mine if you share yours," she says. "The answer is no, and no. Once they knew I was a dyke, I never saw them again."

I try to get a hair out of my face with my forearm, not wanting to take off my gloves. She smiles and pulls the hair back behind my ears. "I bet your family misses you. I know I would."

"Your family is missing out," I say. There wasn't much point in dreaming. They were all dead.

She smiles, sadly this time. She hops off the bench, her arm circles my waist. "Maybe in another life," she whispers. "Maybe next time."

—

Black holes appeared like growing pockmarks through the galaxy, then the universe, and at once a mass collision.
A reset of all that had evolved from that one momentous bang, all to begin anew.
One last act of selfishness for a species that only knew how to take.
Now there is only the nothingness.
There is something I have to do.

—

"This is impossible." My voice is filled with awe, even when a part of me shivers with terror. "You actually did it."

She's watching the glass and metal cube, concentrating. She shakes her head, frowning. "No, I didn't."

She sets down her clipboard, leaning closer to the cube, changing angles. "It's not quite right. I can contain it, but can I use it?" She sighs, runs her fingers through her hair, trying to comb out the mats.

I can't understand her frustration. Behind the once-clear glass, there is … blackness. The cube vibrates with the strain. I thought I would be able to see the gravitational pull, waves of something if she were actually able to contain a black hole, even a small one. But it's a dark, never-ending pit that doesn't even reflect the light from the ceiling.

She slumps into the rickety metal chair beside the table, drops her head into her hands. I can see the tremors in her fingers, lingering undernourishment and insomnia taking its toll.

I move to the other side, stand next to her crumpled form. "Let's get you to bed," I say. "Resetting the universe can wait until morning."

—

The black holes, they remind me of black coffee on a Tuesday morning,
when the days were categorized and fit perfectly in little boxes.
My black cat with the tuxedo-white chest, the black spot on half of its nose.
They're the swirling of the dish water down the drain—
there is something I have to do, but it all runs together in my head,
the words 'I can't do this without you' echo,
her touching my face, a soft kiss on my cheek before she too disappeared,
even though we'd promised each other forever.
Her—

—

"I can't promise that. What if it doesn't work?" I say. Tears are running down my cheeks, but I shake my head because *how can she ask me to do this?*

She flings the papers down onto her desk. They scatter, some of them floating to the floor. "Then what was all this for, huh? Just playing around like this is a goddamn cosmic sandbox that means nothing?"

"I think we should be careful. This is more than you and me, we can't decide to destroy everything. What gives us the right?"

She throws up her hands, her anger setting off more tremors. I can see her shoulders quake with them. "What are you afraid of? Being the villain? I'm not asking you to do anything I wouldn't do myself. I can set the switch, I can stop everything, but I need you to start it again."

She leans against the table, rubs her eyes, continues. "Please. Please, I know this is scary, but what's left here for us? For anyone? Humanity tried, we failed, and we have a chance to start again!"

I shake my head, eyes catching the sheets of calculations and theories. I feel uncertainty like sand in my veins, burning.

She moves towards me and grabs my upper arms. She pushes her head against the side of my cheek until our tears and sweat mingle and I can feel her tremors have only gotten worse. *What if she's wrong?*

"You listen to me." I start to protest but she squeezes my arms tight, and I start sobbing again. "There's nothing left anymore. There's you, and me, and nothing. Is that really enough for you? Is that enough for your parents, your brothers, my friends, everyone? Is that enough for the whole goddamn human race to go gently into that good night?"

I choke on my tears, pull her face forward until our eyes are inches apart. "Why can't that be enough? Why can't us be enough?"

She closes her eyes, and I know.

—

There is something I have to do for her, and even though I don't remember her face, I can feel her heart pounding in my rib cage along with my own, and everything comes back all at once.

There is something I have to do.

I push—

with everything I have,

everything I've been given,

everything I could have been.

I can feel the stitches of what holds me together split, but I made her a promise.

In a moment everything contracts,

then expands,

and then—

HELLO READER

Thank you for reading *The Stars Will Guide Us Back*.
It's readers like you that motivate me to keep creating.
Want to keep up to date with all the latest, get inside my head,
and find out what I'm reading?
Join the Sparks Newsletter at RueSparks.com/Links

Please Review This Book

If you enjoyed *The Stars Will Guide Us Back*, please consider leaving
a review on Goodreads. Reviews help other readers find my books,
and lets me know you're listening.

Where to Find Me

On my website you'll find a bibliography of all my current works,
and news on new releases. You can also connect with me on Twitter
@sparks_writes, Instagram @rue.sparks.makes, or send me an email.
Learn More at RueSparks.com!

THE FABLE OF WREN
COMING OCTOBER 2021

East of the Mississippi and south of the Mason Dixon Line,
the town of Spastoke boasts a devotion to the spotting of a treasured
finch—the Trickster. The smart-mouthed, non-binary Wren is both
a pariah and a prodigy in this city of birdwatchers, their demeanor
keeping everyone but the birds at bay.

After their Uncle Jeremy dies before their eyes, Wren pulls back
emotionally from the world around them. When the body of one
of their fellow birdwatchers is found in the woods, Wren becomes
determined to find the cause. While fighting guilt at the loss of their
uncle, Wren grudgingly accepts the help of the newcomer, Jethro,
as they search for clues to discover what transpired

What they find reveals the town's hidden past, exposing dangers in
the woods steeped in distrust and ruin.

THE DRAGON WARDEN

A queer, genre-bending, fantasy, steampunk, and speculative fiction whirlwind of a web serial.

Achilles has always liked drakes more than humans. These large, but flightless cousins to dragons—or more specifically, their knack at training them—was Achilles' ticket to a comfortable life in the world's center of commerce and industry: the city of Abylone.

Comfort has a cost, one that Achilles isn't willing to accept. Several years after abandoning their life and love at Abylone, Achilles sets out to make things right, with the help of their childhood friend and a crew of misfits from the cloud city of Aerie. But the rising tide of an empire bent on expanding their reign and the age-old mystery of the Old Ones complicates their seemingly simple quest.

Who knew rescuing dragons would be so difficult?

A THANK YOU

To my mother and my little sister Caity for being there for me when I wasn't for myself. To Cam and Carol for emotional support and the wise words when I needed them the most. To Melissa for your compassionate ear when all I can seem to do is complain, and for the many, many desperate pleas for coffee deliveries.

Thank you to Victoria, Charlie, and Cheryl for all the technical and editorial support through the whole process to make the manuscript shine.

And to everyone else in the Twitter #WritingCommunity who came together to make this book possible.

RUE SPARKS
WRITER | ARTIST

A widow, disabled, and a member of the queer community, Rue Sparks traverses the equally harsh and cathartic landscape where trauma and healing align to create stories that burrow into the hearts and minds of their readers.

In addition to *The Stars Will Guide Us Back*, Sparks has authored the novella *Daylight Chasers,* writes the web serial *The Dragon Warden*, and will be releasing the contemporary mystery novel *The Fable of Wren* in 2021. They live in Noblesville, Indiana in the USA with their sweet senior support dog and still draw and paint when they're physically able.